LOVE WILL FIND A WAY

Sara is an hotel receptionist until her friend Caroline, a resident, helps her into a new job — as a secretary at her son Redvers' flower-farming business in the Scillies. When Redvers eventually whispered, 'I love you, Sara', she should have been elated. But an inner voice mocked her — telling her it would have been more truthful had he said, 'I love you, *Miranda*' . . . Was he merely using her as a shield against a love that had once betrayed him?

SUSAN DARKE

LOVE WILL FIND A WAY

Complete and Unabridged

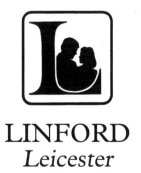

LINFORD
Leicester

First published in Great Britain in 1986 by
Robert Hale Limited
London

First Linford Edition
published 2006
by arrangement with
Robert Hale Limited
London

British Library CIP Data

Darke, Susan
  Love will find a way.—Large print ed.—
  Linford romance library
  1. Scilly, Isles of (England)—Fiction
  2. Love stories 3. Large type books
  I. Title
  823.9'14 [F]

  ISBN 1–84617–338–8

Published by
F. A. Thorpe (Publishing)
Anstey, Leicestershire

Set by Words & Graphics Ltd.
Anstey, Leicestershire
Printed and bound in Great Britain by
T. J. International Ltd., Padstow, Cornwall

1

Sara Ravenscroft stared at the newspaper in stunned surprise. 'Local hero comes home to heartbreak', screamed the headlines. Hardly able to believe her eyes she read avidly on, to find the truth had been distorted out of all knowledge and that she herself was being held responsible for the broken engagement when, in actual fact, the accusation was grossly unfair because the whole thing had been Bernard's fault.

During that terrible time, following a multiple pile-up on the Grand Prix racing track in which her fiancé had been badly injured, she had visited him every day in hospital and, even when she knew he would be paralysed for the rest of his life, her love had never faltered despite the fact that his whole personality had changed almost beyond recognition.

Before the accident he had been sunny-natured and likeable but now he was moody and demanding, continually grumbling and finding fault. She made allowances and, with unfailing optimism, she remained convinced that, once he had become resigned to his disability, his better nature would reassert itself. Together they would build a new life, very different from the one they had planned, but equally rewarding, and she would remain at his side, as his wife and comforter, for all the days of his life.

But Bernard had other ideas. Six months ago he had chosen Sara as his future bride because she was lively and pretty, and the sort of girl who fitted in with the razzmatazz of the racing world, but she was now a perpetual reminder of what might have been and, every time he saw her, his resentment boiled over. He needed somebody as far removed as possible from that other life. Somebody who would remain quietly in the background, ministering to his newly-found ego, and whose sexual needs would never give him cause for jealousy. A plain girl, preferably one with nursing experience, and he had a feeling that Judith Marshall would suit his requirements. She was a State Enrolled nurse, efficient and self-effacing and, as an added bonus, she clearly adored him. During his stay in hospital she had singled him out for special attention and it boosted his morale to have such a devoted slave attending to his every need.

In common with other racing drivers Bernard had been heavily insured, so he would be financially secure for the rest of his life and well able to afford the services of a full-time nurse. He planned to employ Judith in this capacity and, later on, if she gave satisfaction, he would marry her. Meanwhile, Sara was an encumbrance and he was anxious to get rid of her as quickly as possible. But the blame must lie with her and not with him. He wanted everybody to feel sorry for him, and for the whole world to point an accusing finger at the girl whose love was not strong enough to survive the cruel twist of fate which had turned a virile man into a permanent invalid.

With this aim in mind his treatment of her became positively sadistic and, the day before he left hospital, he was so rude and belligerent she almost burst into tears. Finally he accused her of having an affair with Todd Calder, his ex-manager, and, when she hotly denied it, he yelled obscenities at her and demanded the return of her engagement ring. His anger was so violent she was afraid to argue with him and, white faced and trembling, she took the ring off her finger and put it on his bedside table.

'This is your doing, not mine,' she said in a strangled voice. 'I still want to marry you and, if you ever change your mind, you've only got to say the word and I'll come back.'

'Get out of my sight,' he stormed. 'I never want to see you again.'

After she had gone he told the ward sister his sob story, making out that Sara had jilted him in the most heartless possible manner, and soon the news was all round the hospital. Everybody sympathized with him and, on his return home the following day, the local Press gave the broken engagement front-page publicity.

From then onwards Sara's name was mud. The girls at work shunned her, neighbours pretended not to see her, local shopkeepers looked at her with contempt. Even her family were reluctant to accept her version of what had happened and, although her father stood by her, her stepmother continually made snide remarks. At length, in desperation, she decided to leave home.

An old school friend of her mother owned an hotel in Brighton and she was delighted when Sara applied for a job. 'An answer to a prayer, my dear,' she said over the phone. 'My present receptionist is leaving to get married, so come as soon as you like.'

And so it came about that, one sunny morning towards the end of March, Sara Ravenscroft, aged twenty-two, was waiting at Victoria Station for a train to take her to Brighton and to a whole new life. The past was behind her and she would do her utmost to forget the trauma of her broken engagement and the unjust treatment meted out to her by friends, acquaintances and family. Her new job was hundreds of miles from home and there was no reason to suppose she would meet anybody who was aware of the unkind gossip which had well-nigh broken her heart. That page of her life was closed for ever and a fresh chapter was about to begin.

The train was not too crowded and she found a seat by the window without much difficulty. Here she settled herself comfortably, with her possessions spread out around her, and she was leafing through the pages of a magazine when she became aware of a tall presence looming over her. Startled, she glanced up and saw the compartment had filled up and the seat beside her was the only vacant place left.

'I'm so sorry,' she said in some confusion, and she hastily made room for the newcomer who rewarded her with a wintry smile before burying himself behind a newspaper. Clearly he was not going to give her the opportunity to talk. Not that she had any intention of doing so because his autocratic manner was intimidating to the extreme, and she was far too sensitive to risk a rebuff.

Nonetheless, she could not resist stealing an occasional glance at him and she was intrigued by what she saw. Judging by his inflexible mouth and jutting-out jaw, he was one of those strong, silent types who drive a hard bargain. In his early thirties, he was physically and mentally at his peak, a man born to be a leader and who would have no patience with human frailty. Therefore it was with a sense of shock that she saw his right hand was badly scarred as if from some terrible burn, and she wondered what accident could have caused such a crippling disfigurement.

The movement of his fingers had been affected and this was made apparent by the clumsiness with which he turned the pages of the newspaper. She bit her lip in sympathy and, sensing her eyes were on him, he made an impatient movement, half turning his back on her. Scarlet in the face, she stared out of the window, concentrating on the flat countryside where almond trees were in bloom and hedges beginning to show a hint of green.

Arriving at their destination he got out of the train before she did and he was ahead of her in the queue waiting for a taxi. She heard him speak to the driver who immediately shouted out the name of the hotel to the waiting passengers in the hope of picking up another fare, but nobody came forward so the man behind her gave her a shove and told her to get a move on.

'That's your hotel, isn't it?' he said, looking at the label on her suitcase.

'Yes, it is,' she admitted and, feeling extremely selfconscious, she got into the taxi and seated herself as far away as possible from the other passenger, who acknowledged her presence with the briefest of nods.

He had no luggage so he was first out of the taxi and, having paid the driver, he stode into the hotel without a backward glance. Sara followed slowly, not wishing to impose on somebody who obviously wanted to keep her at arm's length and, after the taxi had driven off, she surveyed the exterior of the stone-built Victorian building which was to be her future home.

Situated on the seafront it was conveniently near the beach and shops, and the early spring sunshine had tempted a number of elderly residents to stroll along the promenade. They were well wrapped up against the cold east wind, but the sea sparkled and the well-tended flower beds were already a blaze of colour. Sara decided she was going to be happy here and, wasting no more time, she pushed open the swing doors and entered the hotel foyer.

She received a warm greeting from Evelyn Benson who took her upstairs to an attic bedroom which was rather cramped and sparsely furnished. 'We call it the crow's nest,' Evelyn told her, a trifle apologetically. 'All the best rooms are allocated to the guests, but I hope you'll be comfortable here.'

'I'm going to love it,' Sara assured her and, dumping her suitcase on the bed, she went over to the dormer window to look at the view.

'You'll soon learn to pick out the landmarks,' Evelyn remarked, coming to stand beside her. 'Brighton's a nice place to live, and very convenient for London, which is probably why it's so popular. We're usually fully booked, winter as well as summer. Mostly a roving population, but we do have one resident who lives here all the year round. A Mrs Armstrong. Quite a character but very pleasant.'

She remained chatting for a few minutes and then took her departure, leaving Sara to unpack and freshen up. 'Come downstairs when you're ready,' she said, 'and I'll show you the ropes before lunch. Things are fairly quiet at the moment so you'll have a chance to get settled in before the week-end rush begins.'

The previous receptionist had been extremely efficient and, with Evelyn's assistance, Sara quickly grasped the essentials of her new job. Much to her relief there appeared to be nothing beyond her capabilities and her initial feelings of nervousness soon wore off. However, the morning had been rather a strain and she was glad of a break when Evelyn told her the diningroom was now empty and they could enjoy a belated lunch at a small corner table which was reserved for them.

In point of fact, one of the other tables was still occupied. A middle-aged lady and Sara's unfriendly travelling companion were deep in conversation and they showed no sign of being aware that a tired waitress was hovering in their vicinity.

'Mrs Armstrong, our resident guest,' Evelyn informed her in a confidential undertone. 'That is her son with her. He lives in the Scilly Isles and he comes to see her about once a month. Poor man, he was terribly burnt in a plane crash some time ago.'

'How dreadful!' Sara exclaimed. 'We travelled together on the train and I noticed his hand was badly scarred.'

'He's something of a hero,' Evelyn continued. 'Apparently he was thrown clear but he went back to rescue the pilot, which is how he sustained those terrible burns. He was travelling in one of those light aircraft you see buzzing around. Horrible, dangerous things — they ought not to be allowed. The accident happened in bad weather and I believe the plane crashed into a hillside and burst into flames.'

'Did Mr Armstrong save the pilot's life?' Sara asked.

'Fortunately, yes, otherwise his injuries would have been all in vain. But it is sad how the accident has changed his life.'

'In what way?' Sara was not usually curious about people's backgrounds but for some unknown reason she was intrigued by this man whose attitude towards herself had been curt almost to the point of rudeness. Despite their short acquaintance she had a feeling their destinies ran side by side and, for the life of her, she could not keep a note of eagerness out of her voice.

'Well, for one thing, he had to change his job,' Evelyn replied. 'He trained as an architect but his right hand is now, to all intents and purposes, completely useless. Naturally he was unable to continue with his chosen profession and, according to his mother, this was a bitter blow to him.'

'It must have been,' Sara sympathized. 'Those years of study and hard work — all for nothing. How did he cope?'

'Well, you know the old saying when one door closes another opens. That's how it was with Mr Armstrong. He went to the Scilly Isles to recuperate and while he was there he made friends with a market gardener who was on the verge of bankruptcy. To cut a long story short he went into partnership with him and they are now running a very prosperous market garden.'

'So everything turned out all right,' Sara remarked with a smile. 'I'm glad about that, though I must say he doesn't look a particularly happy man. I wonder why.'

'I gather his ex-fiancée is to blame for the change in him,' Evelyn told her. 'Things looked very bleak after the accident. He'd got no job and, to start with, it seemed likely he might lose his right hand. Anyway, the girl took fright and broke off the engagement. Mrs Armstrong is very bitter about it and she hasn't got a good word to say for Miranda.'

'Miranda?' Sara repeated. 'That's an unusual name.'

Evelyn gave her a considering look. 'The funny thing is, you're a bit like her,' she said. 'The same colouring and height. You could easily be sisters. Perhaps,' she added half jokingly, 'Mr Armstrong will fall for *you*. Don't they say a man is always attracted by the same type of looks?'

'I would have thought it would be a case of once bitten twice shy,' Sara said. 'Perhaps my likeness to Miranda is the reason he treated me so snootily on the train. I certainly got the impression I wasn't his number one pin-up.'

'First impressions can be misleading,' Evelyn declared. 'When he gets to know you better he'll find your likeness to Miranda is only skin deep. I'm sure *you* would never behave in such a heartless manner.'

Sara's colour rose. She hadn't told Evelyn why she had been so anxious to leave home, so the older woman hadn't a clue that she and Miranda had more in common than a mere physical likeness. It was strange that their backgrounds should run on parallel lines, and it was possible that Miranda was no more to blame than she was for her broken engagement. Perhaps she, too, had been forced into the same situation, and Mr Armstrong had insisted on the return of his ring. But surely *his* case was rather different? Bernard's injuries had left him a physical wreck, a helpless invalid who would never be able to consummate a marriage, whereas Mr Armstrong was still a virile man who had quickly built up a new life for himself. Any girl in her right senses would be happy to marry him and it would have been totally unnecessary for him to release Miranda from their engagement. Therefore the move must have come from his fiancée and this would account for Mr Armstrong's unfriendly attitude towards the female sex.

The *young* female sex, she amended,

because he was clearly extremely fond of his mother, and Sara could hardly fail to notice the heart-warming smile he bestowed on Evelyn — to the studied exclusion of herself — when he eventually rose from the dining-table and left the room.

She was kept busy for the rest of the day, receiving telephone calls and making bookings, exchanging pleasantries with the guests as they came and went, and generally making herself useful. Evelyn expressed herself well pleased with the behaviour of her new receptionist and, when Sara eventually retired for the night, she was able to rest assured that she had successfully coped with every eventuality.

The ensuing days fell into a well-ordered pattern and in many ways it was a more rewarding job than that of office typist. For one thing there was far more variety, and it suited Sara's temperament to take responsibility.

Little by little she regained her self-confidence. Nobody in Brighton knew about that unhappy episode in her life when she had been unjustly accused of callous behaviour towards a man who had lost everything worth living for. As far as she knew the broken engagement had only been publicized in the local Press and, although her name and picture had been printed on the front page, it was hardly likely that anybody outside the area would have got to hear about it.

Mrs Armstrong turned out to be a rather domineering woman who, as a resident guest, expected and received preferential treatment. In common with other members of the staff Sara stood slightly in awe of her, and she was surprised, and a little flattered, to find she was being singled out for attention. The older woman's attitude was dictatorial and rather arrogant — she prided herself on belonging to the 'upper crust' — but there was no doubt she had taken a fancy to the pretty, self-effacing girl whose pleasant manners contrasted favourably with those

unlikeable women's libbers she had had
the misfortune to come in contact with.
Miranda Sutcliffe had been one such
girl. She had treated her future
mother-in-law with no love and little
respect, and Caroline Armstrong had
shed no tears when the engagement was
broken off. If fate had not stepped in
she would have done her utmost to
rescue her son from Miranda's clutches
and, from her point of view, it was the
one good thing that had come out of
the accident. He was well rid of her and
now it was up to his mother to find a
suitable girl. One who could be trusted
not to break his heart all over again,
whose disposition was so sweet and
biddable that Caroline would be able to
keep her under her thumb. From the
little she had seen of Sara she was
convinced that here was someone who
would suit the part and, in her usual
forthright manner, she made up her
mind to go to any lengths to bring her
plan to fruition.

Naturally Sara hadn't got an inkling

about the machinations going on behind the aristocratic features of her new friend. Indeed, she couldn't help feeling sorry for Mrs Armstrong who confided in her that she had had to give up her home when she became a widow. She had lived on a beautiful estate in Sussex where her husband had run a riding-school, but it would have been foolish to stay there on her own, so she had sold up and come to Brighton.

'One has to be philosophical about these things,' she sighed. 'Of course I miss living under my own roof and I have to put up with a certain lack of freedom and privacy but, all things considered, I have nothing to grumble about. This hotel suits me very well and Miss Benson is a jewel beyond price.'

'Yes,' Sara agreed. 'She is very kind.'

'How did you hear about the post of receptionist?' Mrs Armstrong continued. 'Miss Benson tells me you come from Bristol — I'm surprised you chose a place so far from home.'

Sara coloured. 'I wanted to get right away,' she prevaricated. 'After my mother died my father re-married and things haven't been too easy.'

Caroline nodded sympathetically. 'The old, old story,' she remarked. 'Cinderella and the wicked stepmother. You did the wisest thing, my dear, but I'm sure you miss your father. Still, you're young enough to make new friends. I gather you have no emotional entanglements?'

Sara's colour deepened. The probing question reopened an unhealed wound but she had no intention of discussing her love life with this inquisitive lady. With a light laugh she held out her left hand for inspection, confident that the pale mark once apparent on her engagement finger was no longer visible. 'Heart whole and fancy free,' she said flippantly.

'I guessed as much,' Caroline remarked with satisfaction and, with elaborate casualness, she changed the subject, though not before Sara had caught a calculating gleam in her eye.

A few days later she announced that her son was due for his monthly visit, a date she looked forward to with the greatest anticipation.

'He's very devoted to you, isn't he?' Sara remarked when she heard the news.

'Yes, he's a dear boy,' Caroline agreed. 'I wish he could come and see me more often but his work keeps him fully occupied. Still, I mustn't grumble. I hear from him once a week, as regular as clockwork. Now, let me see, Thursday is one of your days off, isn't it? I wonder if you would like to join us on a little outing? We could hire a car and take you on a tour of the countryside.' Sara started to protest but the older woman held up her hand in an imperious gesture. 'I would like to show you my old home,' she continued. 'Redvers was born there and, like me, he has a very great affection for the place.'

'I would feel like an intruder,' Sara stammered. 'I'm sure the two of you would rather be on your own.'

'Nonsense,' Caroline declared. 'Young company is just what Redvers needs.'

Sara made another attempt to wriggle out of what could be an embarrassing situation. 'He's probably got lots of girl friends in the Scilly Isles,' she ventured, 'or at any rate one in particular.'

Caroline shook her head. 'He would have told me,' she said with sublime self-confidence. 'Redvers has no secrets from his mother.'

'Who are you trying to kid?' Sara wanted to say. The idea of the strong, silent Redvers confiding the innermost secrets of his soul to his mother, of all people, was almost laughable.

'I planned to do some shopping,' she said half heartedly. Truth to tell she was torn between the desire to get better acquainted with Redvers and the certain knowledge that he would be furious at having a girl fobbed off on him.

'Surely it could wait till another

time?' Caroline asked. 'In any case you could do your shopping early in the morning. I think the best arrangement will be for us to pick you up around twelve o'clock — shall we say by the pier? I have an appointment with my solicitor at eleven-thirty and it hardly seems worth while to go all the way back to the hotel. We can have a pub lunch somewhere on the way to Abbotsfield and get back in plenty of time for Redvers to catch his usual train to London.'

Sara felt she was being bulldozed into a situation which could be fraught with difficulty. 'Your son might object . . . ' she said, her voice trailing off into uncertainty.

'It will be a nice surprise for him', Caroline assured her, 'and a treat for me. I'm really looking forward to having a little outing. At my age life can be rather dull,' she added wistfully. 'Seeing Abbotsfield again will revive old memories. Did I tell you I lived there all my life, even before I was married? I was a Miss Redvers and Abbotsfield belonged to the Redvers family way back in the eighteen hundreds. Unfortunately my poor brother died before he was thirty, so there are none of us left now, except my son.'

'Is that why you called him 'Redvers'?' Sara asked. 'It's rather sad when these old family names die out.'

'I'm glad you think like that,' Caroline said, wiping a nostalgic tear from her eye. 'Most young people nowadays are so unsentimental. Even my son has no sense of history, but I suppose he is making history for himself by putting down new roots in the Scilly Isles.'

'Do you ever feel you'd like to go and live with him?' Sara enquired.

'Perhaps I will one day,' Caroline replied. 'Near him, at any rate, if not actually in the same house. I wouldn't want to share a home with a daughter-in-law, however much I loved her. It's a difficult relationship and often leads to trouble.'

Sara nodded. She knew from personal experience that other relationships could be difficult too and she felt no regret at having cut loose from family ties. Ever since her father re-married, she had been odd man out, because her stepmother very firmly ruled the roost. Indeed, she would have left home years ago if it hadn't been for the very real affection she felt for her father whose second marriage was not a great success.

Twelve o'clock on Thursday found Sara waiting in some trepidation by the pier and her worst fears were realized when she saw the stony look on Redvers's face.

'Good girl,' Caroline gushed. 'I knew you could be relied on not to keep us waiting. Actually, I've only just broken the news to Redvers that you're coming with us. By the way, it's high time you were properly introduced. Previously you have only met *en passant* as it were, but I'm sure you're going to be good friends.'

'Mother is the eternal optimist,'

Redvers remarked, with a degree of curtness in his voice that caused Sara's cheeks to flood with colour. She little knew how attractive she looked, with her wind-blown hair framing her delicate face, and wide-set eyes — were they blue or green? — staring appealingly at him. Miranda had looked like that when he first met her but he had soon discovered her apparent naivety masked an acquisitive nature. If things didn't work out exactly as she wanted them to, she would raise merry hell, and he would never forget her cruel words when she flung his ring back at him after the dreadful accident — the memory of which still gave him nightmares.

'Marry a cripple?' she had exclaimed. 'Not me. I never could bear physical deformity and your hand gives me the shudders every time I look at it.'

She had been very young, only twenty, spoilt and selfish to a marked degree, but with a beauty of face and figure he had never come across since.

Never — until now. Meeting Sara in the train, sharing a taxi with her from the station to the hotel, had been a nerve-wracking experience and had revived bitter-sweet memories. Her likeness to Miranda was so strong it was almost uncanny, but he had vowed he would never again be taken in by a pretty face and, even though Sara's proximity caused his heartbeats to quicken and the blood to boil in his veins he was determined not to pursue the acquaintance.

Therefore his anger at having Sara foisted off on him was perfectly understandable and he gave vent to his feelings by behaving in a manner that was both rude and boorish. Caroline either did not — or pretended not to — notice, and her flow of small talk never faltered. Sara did her best to back her up but presently she lost patience with Redvers and, when they had finished lunch, she took advantage of Caroline's visit to the powder room to give her host a piece of her mind.

'I think your behaviour is absolutely abominable,' she told him. 'Don't you realize you're spoiling your mother's enjoyment of a day she's been looking forward to for ages? And, if you think I wangled an invitation just to get to know you better — I didn't, so you needn't flatter yourself. When I saw you in the train I thought you were the most arrogant and unfriendly man I'd ever met and to-day hasn't changed my opinion in the slightest.'

She paused to draw breath, and found that he was surveying her with a quizzical expression on his face, almost as if he was looking at her with new eyes. 'How handsome he is,' she thought distractedly. A strong face, dark and brooding, with winged eyebrows as black as a raven's wing. His tanned skin gave him a healthy, outdoor look, and his well-muscled body bore witness to his fine physical condition. But it was his mouth that drew her attention. Firmly moulded, it turned upward at the corners, denoting a nature that was less stubborn and dogmatic than one would have thought, and she found herself wondering what it would feel like to have those very masculine lips pressed against hers.

What had come over her, she wondered. She had never felt like this with Bernard, never been wafted on wings of ecstasy by his rather clumsy embraces. How different it would be with Redvers. His love-making would be rough yet gentle, arousing all her primitive instincts and taking her with him to realms of unbelievable bliss.

These unbridled thoughts ran through her mind like quicksilver and it required a conscious effort of will to hold them in check. She knew it would antagonize Redvers still further if he guessed the real reason for her heightened colour, so she flung her head back and stared at him with stormy eyes. After a moment he shrugged his shoulders and acknowledged defeat.

'Very well, Miss Ravenscroft.' he said, with a certain melting of his hitherto icy manner. 'I get your point. For my mother's sake I'll behave towards you with a modicum of politeness.' The hint of a smile crossed his face. 'I really have been rather rude to you, so please accept my apologies.'

When Caroline returned from the powder room she immediately sensed a different atmosphere and she visibly relaxed. She knew how difficult Redvers could be and, earlier on, it had seemed likely that her little plan was going to misfire. But now all was well and she smiled benignly on the two young people as they made their way out to the hired car in readiness for their visit to her beloved Abbotsfield.

2

The manor house, a large stone-built residence, had belonged to the Redvers family since the early eighteen hundreds. It was now a private nursing-home and, judging by the well-tended gardens, and general air of affluence, a very successful one. The riding-school had been sold separately and considerable activity was going on in the stable yard as a party of schoolchildren arrived in a minibus, pushing and shoving each other in their eagerness to renew acquaintance with their favourite mount.

'It must be the start of the summer term,' Caroline exclaimed. 'Chessington School — I recognize their hatbands. I was a pupil there when I was a girl,' she continued chattily. 'It seems only yesterday that I wore a navy blue gym slip and blazer, but I fear a lot of water has flowed under the bridges since then. Ah me! How I wish I could turn the clock back and be a child again.'

'Now, Mother, don't get sentimental,' Redvers admonished. 'I'm sure your schooldays were *not* the happiest days of your life. Many people tend to view the past through rose-coloured spectacles but personally I prefer to look forward, not back.'

'Does it bother you that Abbotsfield is no longer your home?' Sara asked.

'Not in the slightest,' he replied. 'Of recent years the upkeep had become an increasing burden and we were lucky to get a good price for it.'

'I told you he wasn't sentimental, didn't I?' Caroline asked, turning to Sara with an expressive shrug. 'I surmise that *you*, on the other hand, would be heart-broken at the idea of leaving an ancestral home.'

'I've never been in that position,' Sara answered with a smile. 'Strictly middle-class — that's my family background, though I won't say I haven't had my dreams of glory.'

'That's nothing to be ashamed of,' Caroline said, giving her hand an affectionate pat. 'I'm sure Cinderella indulged in wishful thinking long before she met Prince Charming. And, sooner or later, Prince Charming will come along for *you*, my dear, I'm quite sure of that.'

Before she could stop herself, Sara's glance flew towards Redvers and she was covered with confusion when she found herself being subjected to a very penetrating stare. Surely he didn't think that her idle remark about dreams of glory had any special significance? It would be too shame-making if he believed she was cultivating a friendship with wealthy Caroline Armstrong for the express purpose of ensnaring her highly eligible son. She looked hastily away, her tell-tale colour denoting her embarrassment.

'Well, Mother,' he said after a moment, 'Have you seen all you want to see, or are there any places of special significance you want to visit? I'm sure Matron will raise no objection if we stroll through the grounds.'

'Yes, Redvers, that would be nice,' Caroline replied. 'It's not as if we shall be intruding on a private residence.'

'Is this the first time you have visited your old home since you left?' Sara asked in surprise. After all, Abbotsfield was only thirty miles from Brighton and she would have thought Caroline would have wanted to revive old memories long before this.

'Leaving Abbotsfield was rather like suffering a bereavement,' Caroline explained. 'It was weeks before I could bring myself to visit my husband's grave, and I felt the same way about Abbotsfield. Fortunately time is a great healer and I have had six months in which to learn to adjust.'

'I don't know why, but I quite thought you had been living in Brighton for ages,' Sara remarked.

'One of the fixtures in the hotel?'

Caroline smiled. 'I suppose I do give that impression — possibly because I'm the only permanent resident.'

'Must it be permanent?' Redvers interrupted. 'I've been on at you ever since you left Abbotsfield to come and live in the Scillies, but you're so confoundedly independent.'

'I've lived in Sussex all my life,' Caroline pointed out, 'and I'm not quite ready yet to leave my native shores. Besides, would you really want me living on your doorstep? You had your own flat in London long before you went to the Scilly Isles, and you only condescended to come home for occasional week-ends.'

'Well, you know Dad and I didn't exactly hit it off,' Redvers reminded her. 'Looking back I can see it was more my fault than his, but that's old history and I'm sure Sara isn't interested in our reminiscences.'

Parking the car on the grass verge by the side of the road, he got out and opened the wrought-iron gates. A long drive ran as straight as an arrow towards the gracious house that had once been Redvers's home and, as her glance travelled up the broad flight of steps to the open front door, she felt that she was being invited in.

She felt Redvers's hand on her arm. 'Wake up,' he said. 'It's foolish to indulge in dreams of glory in this day and age. You see before you a private nursing-home, run by a board of directors strictly on the make. I assure you the patients have to pay through the nose for the privilege of dying in such elegant surroundings.'

For an hour or more they strolled through the grounds without meeting anybody, and Caroline was in her element, bringing various features to Sara's attention: a copse of silver birch trees where soon the bluebells would be in bloom, a rustic bridge spanning a babbling brook, and a small classical temple set at the edge of a pool.

'This is where my husband proposed to me,' she reminisced. 'He was a friend of my brother and he had come on a week-end visit. I was never more surprised in my life when he asked me to marry him, for we hardly knew each other, but it was a case of love at first sight and I suppose that was what made it so romantic.'

'Mother, will you please stop?' Redvers said. 'Can't you see you're embarrassing our guest? You'll have to be careful, Sara,' he added, 'or she'll be boring you with the family snapshot album.'

'I wouldn't be bored — I love family photographs,' Sara replied, 'and I love hearing about what happened in the olden days.'

'The *olden* days?' he repeated with a quizzical smile. 'That puts you well and truly in your place, doesn't it, Mother?'

'Oh, I didn't mean . . . ' Sara protested, scarlet in the face, and then broke off in relief because they were both laughing at her discomfiture.

'I'm afraid it's time to go,' Redvers said, glancing at his watch. 'You don't want to be late for your evening meal and I have a train to catch.'

★   ★   ★

During the next few weeks Sara's horizons began to widen. She was medium good at tennis so she had no difficulty in joining a club where the members welcomed her with casual friendliness.

Occasionally she swam in the sea but it was early in the season and the water was still very cold. Running back to the hotel to get her circulation going again, she could not imagine she would ever be brave enough to join the hardy band of Christmas Day swimmers.

Thursdays and Mondays were her days off and her hours were not too long, though they varied from day to day. Sometimes she worked till late at night but at other times she would finish early, so, taking it all in all, she had a considerable amount of spare time, and quite a lot of it she devoted to

Caroline who was delighted to have the companionship of such a pretty and lively girl.

Now that she was safely out of range of snide remarks and pointing fingers, Sara was able to relax, and she became once more the happy-natured person she had been before Bernard's tragic accident. She was popular with everybody, staff and guests alike, but although several men showed more than a passing interest in her she refused to let herself be drawn into anything more serious than a light flirtation.

Caroline watched with approval. The more she saw of Sara the more she was convinced she had found the right girl for Redvers. She was not quite out of the 'top drawer', as Miranda had been, but she was one of nature's gentle-women, and, by virtue of her pleasing manners and attractive speaking voice, she would be able to hold her own in any situation. Miranda, of course, had the advantage of a more moneyed background and there was a trace of blue blood in her veins, but nowadays all that sort of thing went by the board.

Now that she had got her son's future satisfactorily mapped out Caroline looked forward impatiently to his next visit and she was disappointed when he wrote to say he would not be able to get away till the middle of June. This would be a six-week gap instead of the usual four and she fretted at the delay. She even wondered if she could think up some excuse to bring him to Brighton at an earlier date but she hesitated to feign illness in case she brought retribution upon herself. She was uncomfortably aware of the fact that she suffered from high blood pressure and, if the gods chose to retaliate, a genuine heart attack would be in the nature of poetic justice. So she would have to 'hold her horses', as her husband had been fond of saying and, in the meantime, she would get to know Sara better.

With this end in view she arranged as

many little jaunts as possible and, when Sara protested that she was being thoroughly spoilt, she put forward the unanswerable argument that she could not go to these places on her own and that Sara was doing her a favour by giving her the pleasure of her company. 'And the next time Redvers comes,' she promised, 'we'll go to Abbotsfield again.'

Meanwhile she had to be content with his letters and she enjoyed reading excerpts to Sara who soon built up a picture of the Isles, the life, the scenery and the people, because Redvers filled many pages with vivid descriptions.

'From where I am sitting I can see the whole magnificent sweep of the bay. To-day it is a beautiful Mediterranean blue, dotted with red hulled fishing boats. The offshore islands are pencil clear — too clear for my reckoning because I believe it will rain to-morrow and I was planning to get on with the building of a drystone wall. As you know, I am strictly a fine weather gardener and, on wet days, I prefer to be working in the greenhouses.'

'Since coming to the Scilly Isles I have learnt a lot about birds — quite a lot anyway. I can now distinguish between a Ringed Plover and an Oyster-Catcher, a Gannet and a Shag. Naturally there are plenty of sea birds here. I used to call them all gulls, but now I talk knowledgeably about Guillemots and Razorbills and Cormorants. Did you know a flight of curlews is called a 'concourse'? I didn't until the other day when I was talking to Nathan Bond. Quite a character is old Nathan . . . '

Sara never grew tired of listening and, when she was sorting through the mail, she would pounce eagerly on an envelope bearing a Scillies stamp, knowing there was a treat in store for her when she came off duty.

But one morning there was a letter for Caroline in handwriting Sara did not know. The envelope was pale blue, and the stamp was postmarked

London. What intrigued Sara was that it was addressed to Abbotsfield and had been forwarded on to the hotel so, whoever the writer was, she must have been out of touch with Caroline for some considerable time.

It was not officially Sara's job to carry in Caroline's breakfast tray but the dining-room staff were always rushed off their feet, so they had been delighted when the new receptionist offered to take over this chore. 'I know it's lazy of me to have breakfast in bed but I like to read my newspaper without interruption', Caroline explained. 'If there's one thing I complain about in hotel life it's the lack of privacy. Some people are bright-eyed and bushy-tailed first thing in the morning, but I'm afraid I'm not at my best till the more civilized hour of ten a.m. If I want to spoil myself, why not? I'm well enough off to pay for my privileges.'

On this particular morning there was only the one letter reposing on the breakfast tray and Caroline frowned as

44

she picked it up. Holding it between thumb and forefinger she made no attempt to open it and she remained unusually silent while Sara fetched her bedjacket and plumped up her pillows.

'What's the matter?' Sara asked in some concern. 'Aren't you feeling well?'

'This letter!' Caroline exclaimed in a strangled voice. 'I'm very much afraid it's from Miranda.'

All the colour had drained from her face and she looked suddenly older and very vulnerable. Sara moved the tray to one side and, sitting on the edge of the bed, she patted the older woman's hand.

'Please don't upset yourself,' she begged.

'Upset myself?' Caroline repeated distractedly. 'If that wretched girl hopes to come back into my son's life, I'll do all in my power to stop her. You don't know her, Sara, but she's rotten — rotten to the core — and I never understood why Redvers allowed himself to be trapped into an engagement.

Her fatal charm, I suppose, because, on the surface she is a taking little creature, but it is only a façade. When I got to know her better I came to hate her — yes, hate her. If Redvers had married her I tremble to think what his future would have been. And now she has the audacity to write to me!' She looked at the letter with revulsion and would have torn it up if Sara had not restrained her.

'Don't do that,' she advised. 'See what she says and then you can act accordingly.'

'Yes, you're right,' Caroline agreed, and she seized a knife from the breakfast tray and savagely slit open the envelope. '*So!*' she exclaimed, glancing at the address at the top of the page. 'She's staying at a hotel in London, is she? The last I heard of her was nearly a year ago when she was married to a wine merchant and living in Bristol. I suppose I shall have to read what she says but be a dear and pour me out a cup of coffee first. I have a feeling I shall need something to sustain me.'

In silence Sara did as she was told and, while Caroline slowly sipped the aromatic liquid, she did her best to hide her impatience. What could Miranda be writing about, she wondered. Perhaps her marriage had broken up and she was regretting her decision not to marry Redvers. She was two years older now and she would have forgotten the revulsion she felt at the sight of her fiancé's badly injured hand.

If this should prove to be the case there was nothing either Caroline or Sara could do to prevent a reconciliation and it was with a feeling of impending doom that Sara waited for the letter to be read aloud.

As it turned out her worst fears were realized. Miranda's marriage *had* broken up and she was anxious to get in touch with Redvers again. 'He is the only man I have ever truly loved,' the letter continued. 'I admit I behaved badly at a time when he needed me most, but I am older and wiser now and surely it is not too late to make amends? Marrying Ronnie was the biggest mistake of my life. He is an alcoholic and I am divorcing him on the grounds of extreme cruelty. The decree will shortly be made absolute and then I will be free to marry Redvers. I hoped to be able to contact him in London but apparently he sold the flat soon after we parted and it has changed hands since then and the new owner hasn't a clue where he is. Dear Caroline, I beg you to tell me Redvers's present whereabouts. I am sure he still cares for me and there is no reason why our ill-starred romance should not have a happy ending.'

With a look of fury on her face, Caroline tore the letter into tiny shreds. '*Dear Caroline*, indeed! How dare she!' she cried with a vehemence which boded ill for her blood pressure. 'If she expects a reply from me she'll have to wait till the cows come home. Never, under any circumstances, will I give her Redvers's address. Thank God he is living in the Scilly Isles — it will make it more difficult for her to trace him.'

Sara was so upset by the contents of Miranda's letter that all she wanted to do was to fly to her 'crow's nest' and burst into tears, but duty called and she found solace in working non-stop for the rest of the morning. Her programme was always a full one and, fortunately, today was extra busy, for there were a number of problems to be sorted out, calling for tact and initiative, two qualities very necessary for ensuring the smooth running of an hotel. Long before lunchtime her worry about Miranda had faded into the background and, when she joined Evelyn Benson in the dining-room for their belated meal, she was able to greet her with her customary smile.

'You will have heard all about the fair Miranda reappearing like a blot on the landscape,' Evelyn remarked as they sat down and made a start on the delicious Sole Véronique which had been saved back for them. 'Caroline has worked herself up into a terrible state, phoning the Matron at Abbotsfield and laying down the law. Talk about Queen Victoria on the rampage! It's really quite exciting, isn't it? I can't wait to see what will happen now.'

3

Sara happened to be off duty when Miranda's second letter arrived, so she knew nothing about it until she came downstairs at around ten o'clock to find Caroline waiting for her in the foyer.

'I have had another letter from Miranda,' she announced, 'again re-addressed from Abbotsfield. I gather she's been in touch with Matron who, I'm glad to say, refused to give her my address. Apparently she can't understand why I don't wish to see her, though I would have thought the reason would be obvious, even to someone as thick-skinned as Miranda. However, I've decided to change my tactics. I shall write and tell her Redvers is in Canada, travelling from place to place with a trade delegation, and that he'll be abroad for the next six months. Even Miranda will hardly go all that way on a

51

wild-goose chase.'

The enormity of the lie left Sara speechless but Caroline seemed unaware of the condemnation in the girl's eyes. 'I quite realize Redvers will be furious if he finds out,' she continued. 'He's like my father — he cannot bear interference, but he has to be protected from himself. He cared very deeply for Miranda and he has never looked at another girl since she threw him over, but she's shallow and selfish and I will *not* stand aside and allow him to make a fool of himself for a second time.'

'Six months doesn't last for ever,' Sara reminded her. 'What will you do at the end of that time if Miranda is still of the same mind?'

''Sufficient unto the day is the evil thereof',' Caroline quoted. 'I hope Redvers will meet and fall in love with another girl long before then. At any rate it will get Miranda out of our hair for the time being and that is all to the good. Run along now, my dear. You want to make the most of this lovely sunshine.'

Sara was wearing her bikini under her beach coat and, as she wended her way down to the beach, she was in a thoughtful mood. If Redvers had cared as deeply for Miranda as his mother implied, then it was a foregone conclusion that, sooner or later, they would get together again, and she herself would be left out on a limb. She did not approve of Caroline's methods but evidently Miranda was a spoilt and shallow creature and unworthy of Redver's love, so she could not condemn Caroline for doing her utmost to keep them apart. It was the thought of Redvers's anger should he discover what his mother had done that frightened her. A rift between them would break Caroline's heart because he was all in all to her and, without his love and support, she would face a lonely old age. However, there was nothing Sara could do about it. Caroline had chosen what course she was going to take and she would allow nothing or nobody to stand in her way.

The beach was already crowded, the summer-like weather having tempted many people out of doors. Sara spotted two members of the tennis club, nice girls, a little older than herself, both with a toddler in tow. They were comfortably ensconced on lilos, and beckoned Sara to come and join them.

'Oh, the bliss!' one of them exclaimed. 'Why can't it always be summer?'

'Aren't I lucky it's my day off?' Sara replied, sitting down beside them and discarding her beach coat. 'You girls have got it made. Your life's one long holiday.'

'Hark at her! She must be joking!' Claudia exclaimed. 'I haven't had a moment's peace since Jeremy was born.'

'He's gorgeous, isn't he?' Sara replied. 'Like a Botticelli cherub. I do envy you.'

'The time will come, my girl, and all too soon,' Isobel forecast, with a note of doom in her voice. 'No engagement ring, I see, but surely there's a man in the offing?'

Sara shook her head. 'Not at the

moment,' she said lightly, 'but there are one or two very attractive men at the tennis club.'

'You can have your pick as long as you keep your thieving hands off my Philip,' Claudia giggled. 'You'd better watch it, Bel. Your Chris has always had an eye for a pretty girl.'

'Not since Dulcibel was born,' Isobel answered, gazing fondly at her chubby offspring who was busily filling a bucket with pebbles. 'He's so dotty about her he wouldn't dream of looking at another woman. That's a super bikini you're wearing,' she continued, as Sara proceeded to cover herself with sun-tan lotion. 'Is it strictly for decoration or are you going for a swim?'

'I'll bet it's for decoration,' Claudia said, a shade enviously as she compared Sara's slender figure with her own rather lumpy measurements.

'Well, if you've got assets, why not show them?' asked Isobel who was the proud possessor of a forty-inch bust.

'I think you inherit your shape from

your mother,' Claudia declaimed. 'If she's fat you'll be fat and it's no good fighting against it.'

'I don't agree,' Isobel argued. 'It's a matter of appetite. If you stuff yourself with cream cakes and chocolates, like your mother does, you're bound to end up overweight. I shouldn't let it worry you. Philip obviously loves you plump and cuddly.'

'Yes, he does, doesn't he?' Claudia said complacently, and she took a box of after-eights out of her hold-all and handed them round. 'Left over from last Saturday's dinner party,' she explained, 'so I'm not as piggy as you seem to think I am.'

'That was a super evening,' Isobel remarked. 'I suppose I shall have to stir my stumps and return the compliment.' She turned to Sara. 'I'll phone you some time and perhaps we could fix a date? I'll try to get hold of a spare man — there are quite a few I have in mind who might be suitable.'

Claudia gave Sara a merry wink. 'Be

warned, my friend,' she said. 'Bel's an incorrigible matchmaker and, given half a chance, she'll have you engaged and married before the end of the summer.'

Sara laughed and, jumping to her feet, she seized Jeremy with one hand and Dulcibel with the other. 'Who's coming for a paddle?' she asked.

Such energy was infectious and soon all five of them were running in and out of the water, the toddlers screaming with delight every time a wave caught up with them.

Walking along the promenade on the way to post her letter to Miranda, Caroline glanced down at the beach and happened to catch sight of them. 'I believe that's Sara,' she thought. 'Who can she be with, I wonder? Claudia Bickerstaffe and Isobel Carruthers, unless I'm very much mistaken. Nice girls, both of them. I was at school with Isobel's mother and I know Claudia's husband is very well connected. Thank heaven, I'm not a snob, but I'm glad

Sara knows how to pick and choose her friends.'

She stayed watching the little group for several minutes and then proceeded on her way with a smile of gratification on her face. 'This is going to spike your guns, Miranda,' she said to herself as she posted her letter with a flourish. 'I've got six months to bring my plan to fruition and, if I don't succeed in pulling off a match between Redvers and Sara within that time, then my name isn't Caroline Armstrong.'

Isobel kept her promise and phoned Sara a few days later to arrange a date for her dinner party. 'It will be quite an informal do, only eight of us,' she said, 'so don't wear anything too frightfully glam.'

Sara knew she could rely on Caroline to guide her along the right path and, when she broached the subject, the older woman professed herself delighted to be of help. 'We'll go to Elsa Mettam in Hove,' she decided. 'I have an account there and you can be sure of getting the very best attention. There's nothing she doesn't know about *haute couture*, and she also stocks some quite smart little numbers for the younger set.'

'Won't she be a bit pricey?' Sara asked. She had always been in the habit of shopping at the department stores and the prospect of going to an expensive salon rather daunted her. 'I don't want to blow a week's salary on just one dress.'

'You must let me take care of that,' Caroline smiled. 'As I said, I have an account with Elsa and it will give me the greatest pleasure to pay for your outfit. No, my dear,' she continued as Sara started to protest, 'I'm not going to listen to your objections. I always wanted a daughter but the fates decreed otherwise. I haven't even any nieces so, quite truthfully, you'll be doing me a favour. There's one thing you'll have to learn, Sara — to receive a gift graciously.'

'Then I will,' Sara cried and, with a

spontaneous gesture of gratitude, she gave Caroline a warm, impulsive hug which brought tears of happiness to the older woman's eyes.

The shopping expedition was a great success and it was nearly half-past five before they got back to the hotel and, as Sara was on duty at six, she had a rush to get ready. She hastily unpacked her purchases and, resisting the temptation to try them on straightaway, she had a quick wash and tidy up before hurrying downstairs to take over from Evelyn, who had been kind enough to give her extra time off to go shopping.

'Did you get what you wanted?' Evelyn asked, smiling at the girl's flushed face and general air of excitement.

'Yes, it was super,' Sara answered. 'An absolute dream of a dress. I can't thank you enough for letting me go.'

'Fair's fair,' Evelyn observed. 'You scratch my back and I'll scratch yours. I believe in giving my staff the treatment they deserve. You're a good worker,

Sara, and I'm keeping my fingers crossed that you won't leave me in the lurch — I'd never get a satisfactory replacement in the middle of the season.'

'Not to worry,' Sara said half jokingly. 'I give you my solemn promise not to leave in a hurry.'

'It's very important that you *do* stay,' Evelyn continued on a more serious note. 'You see, my dear, I may have to go into hospital shortly to have an operation for a hiatus hernia. I've been on the waiting list for some time and, if I'm called at a moment's notice, I shall have to go, there's no two ways about it. I have a friend who will hold the fort for me but she'll need all the support and help you can give her.'

'You can rely on me,' Sara vowed. 'I wouldn't dream of letting you down. But I'm dreadfully sorry to hear about your trouble. I had no idea there was anything the matter with you. You're always so cheerful — I think you're an absolute marvel.'

'It doesn't do to moan and groan about these things,' Evelyn replied. 'Nobody loves an invalid. In any case, I'm not really ill but I suffer from a lot of discomfort which can be very wearying, so the sooner it's seen to the better. By the way, this is in the strictest confidence — I don't want any of the guests to hear about it, particularly Mrs Armstrong. She might find it unsettling and decide to decamp to pastures new.'

'I quite understand. I won't breathe a word,' Sara promised and, before anything more could be said, they were interrupted by a telephone call which effectively put an end to any further discussion.

* * *

On the day of the dinner party Isobel phoned to tell Sara she had arranged for Toby Gregson to pick her up at the hotel at seven-thirty and bring her home afterwards. 'You've met him once or twice at the tennis club,' she said.

'Being a sales rep. he doesn't come all that often, but I can vouch for his morals. He's a nice guy and he won't proposition you unless you give him the come-hither.'

'Yes, I have met him,' Sara agreed, remembering the tall, blue-eyed young man with the pleasant out-of-door look. 'I'm glad you didn't choose Mark Hardcastle for my escort,' she added with a laugh. Mark was another member of the tennis club and he had already made several passes at her, apparently impervious to her frigid response.

'Our local Don Juan? I wouldn't do that to you, darling, though actually he *is* coming to-night. I've invited another lone female, an old school friend I haven't seen for umpteen ages, and he'll suit her down to the ground.'

Getting ready for the party Sara couldn't help wishing that Redvers was going to be her partner instead of Toby Gregson. 'One day it will happen', she dreamed. 'One day he will hold me in his arms and whisper that he loves me and then we will be carried on wings of song to unimaginable heights of bliss.'

Behind her in the mirror she fancied she could see his shadowy form, immaculately dressed in an evening suit, with a frilled white shirt and a carnation in his buttonhole and, so vivid was the image, that her heart turned over in her breast. 'Redvers,' she whispered. 'Redvers, my darling, my love . . . please make my dreams come true.'

Toby arrived punctually and, as they walked out to the car, he reminded her they had been opponents on the tennis courts a week or two ago. 'You play a good game,' he remarked, 'though you could do with a bit more practice.'

'I'm not all that dedicated,' she replied. 'It's fun and I enjoy it but I wouldn't want to spend all my spare time on the courts.'

'How are you liking it in Brighton?' he asked. 'Isobel tells me you only came here recently. Where are you from?'

'The west country,' she replied cagily. 'Yes, I like it here very much and my job is super. I used to be a typist in an office but being a hotel receptionist is much less boring, though it's pretty hectic at times and I have to work unsocial hours.'

'Unfortunately I'm only home at week-ends,' he said regretfully, 'but evidently you can occasionally wangle a Saturday night off once in a while, so I hope we'll be able to get together again.'

'I hope so,' she replied non-committally and he was aware of a note of constraint in her voice. So she didn't want to get too involved? A pity because he had taken a definite fancy to her.

Predictably, Isobel lived in an executive-type house and, although she had only been married a couple of years, she was already the possessor of all the things that had once been considered luxuries. Her husband was charming, with the easy, relaxed manners of the true-born gentleman, and he immediately made his guests feel at home. Claudia and Philip had already arrived and a few minutes later Mark Hardcastle made his appearance.

'And where is the unattached female you promised me?' he asked Isobel. 'You said it was to be a surprise and I hoped it might be Sara Ravenscroft, but I see Gregson has already staked his claim.'

'Sara is hardly your type,' Isobel commented. 'You need somebody armour-plated to withstand your charms.'

'It sounds as if you've chosen a Valkyrie or an Amazon,' Mark grumbled. 'Come on, Bel — who is she?'

'I'm not telling,' she said. 'You'll have to wait and see. But I'll give you a clue. She went to school with me and you probably met her at my wedding a couple of years ago.'

'That's a lot of help', he groaned, 'considering there were about four hundred guests.'

Isobel relented. 'Oh, well, I might as well put you in the picture,' she said.

'It's Miranda Sutcliffe. At the time of my wedding she had just broken off her engagement to Redvers Armstrong, though since then she has been married and divorced.'

'Miranda Sutcliffe?' he exclaimed. 'I knew she got married to Ronnie Bingham but I didn't realize she was divorced. So this puts her on the marriage market again. What a bit of luck. I must pull my socks up and reserve a place in the queue. The Sutcliffes are rolling and I could do with a rich wife to fill the coffers.'

'I wouldn't bother,' Isobel said. 'I think she hopes to get Redvers back again.'

Mark raised an eyebrow. 'You surprise me. Wasn't he injured in a plane crash about the time the engagement was broken off? I heard a rumour that his arm was amputated and Miranda refused to marry him because of it.'

'Yes, she took fright and threw Redvers over in favour of Ronnie. A fat lot of good it did her. Ronnie turned out to be an alcoholic and the marriage was a disaster. Ironically Redvers made a good recovery and he's hale and hearty again.'

'So he didn't lose his arm after all?'

'Thankfully, no, but his right hand never fully recovered and he had to give up his job. You may remember he was an architect and he had a brilliant future mapped out.'

'Poor chap.' Apart from Mark's penchant for the girls he wasn't a bad sort of fellow. 'What is he doing now?'

Isobel shrugged. 'I haven't a clue. I've completely lost touch with the family, though I do know Mr Armstrong died last year and that Abbotsfield has been sold. I suppose I could always get news from my mother if I wanted to. She was at school with Caroline and they've kept up an intermittent friendship ever since.'

Mark grinned. 'Good old Chessington. Who didn't go to school there, I wonder?'

'Certainly not any members of the

male sex,' she laughed. 'We were cloistered like nuns but that didn't prevent us getting up to mischief. If the headmistress had known what went on after lights were out her hair would have turned white. We were all boy mad, especially Miranda. Now, I wonder . . . ' She broke off as a sudden thought struck her. 'I wonder if Miranda got in touch with me for the express purpose of finding out more about Redvers. She rang me up a few days ago, angling for an invitation, and she's probably avid for news of her ex-fiancé. She'll be livid when I tell her I don't know a thing.' She paused, her head tilted on one side as she listened to the sound of a car coming up the drive. 'That will be Miranda,' she said. 'All set to make an entrance. I do believe she's always late on purpose.'

4

Sara was the only one present who had not met Miranda and she stood quietly in the background while the others were greeted as old friends.

'How lovely to see you all again', Miranda gushed and, spotting Sara, she singled her out for attention. 'Do I see a stranger in our midst?' she asked. 'Whose property are you? Toby's or Mark's?'

'Neither,' Isobel answered crisply. 'Let me introduce you. This is Sara Ravenscroft. Sara, meet Miranda Sutcliffe — sorry, no — Bingham.'

'Sutcliffe will do,' Miranda told her. 'I intend to forget the 'Bingham' with all speed. Nice to meet you, Sara. It's a funny thing but your face seems strangely familiar. And your name rings a bell. Sara Ravenscroft. It's a good deal more unusual than plain Jane Smith or Susan Jones.'

A wave of giddiness swept over Sara. Was it possible that, by some cruel twist of fate, Miranda had read about Bernard's accident and the subsequent broken engagement? She could see the headlines now, splashed in huge print across the front page. 'Local hero comes home to heartbreak'. And the photograph of herself, taken with Bernard on the occasion of one of his previous triumphs, with one arm round her waist and the other waving aloft a bottle of bubbly. Caroline had mentioned that Miranda had been living in Bristol since her marriage to Ronnie, and this was Sara's home town, so was it beyond the realms of possibility to assume Miranda had read that particular edition of the local newspaper and had retained a hazy memory of what was supposed to have happened?

'I'm sure we haven't met before,' she said firmly, and she felt grateful to Toby who, sensing her discomfiture, filled in the awkward gap with an amusing anecdote about mistaken identities which made them all laugh.

Seated at the dinner table she was able to watch Miranda unobserved and the impression she formed of the girl Redvers had once been engaged to was not at all favourable. 'Hard as nails', she guessed and she felt a bond of sympathy with Caroline who had decided a downright lie was justified if it served to keep Redvers and Miranda apart. Undeniably the girl had charm and, unlike Sara, who was of a more retiring disposition, she simply oozed self-confidence. Also she was as sexy as they come, which Sara certainly was not, and, within minutes of her arrival, she had Christopher, Philip and Mark eating out of her hand. Only Toby seemed impervious to her wiles and, such is the contrariness of human nature, it was towards *him* that she directed the full force of her personality. He parried her overtures with perfect politeness but, for all the progress she made, she might as well have beaten her head against a brick wall.

'Well, you can't win 'em all,' she thought philosophically, but she felt a bit peeved that Sara had apparently enslaved Toby without the slightest trouble. 'Maybe there's more to this girl than meets the eye,' she decided. 'She could be a serious rival if she set her mind to it. Not that I need worry. The only man I'm really interested in is Redvers Armstrong and there's no reason to suppose they'll ever even meet.'

When the meal was over the girls went upstairs to powder their noses and Miranda asked in dulcet tones whether Sara had a job or if she stayed at home to arrange the flowers. 'A receptionist?' she repeated. 'As a matter of interest, which hotel?

Sara would rather not have told her but she could hardly refuse and, in any case, the others knew where she worked and they would think it extremely odd if she tried to hold back the information. What a pity Caroline had already written to Miranda and told her her address. An inquisition was sure to follow and Sara could think of no means of escape.

'One of the hotels on the seafront,' she said, stalling for time.

Miranda pounced. 'Not the Crosby, by any chance?' she asked.

Sara nodded reluctantly and there was a glint of something like triumph in Miranda's eyes. 'That's very interesting,' she said. 'Mrs Armstrong is a resident guest there, isn't she? How do you get on with her?'

'She's very pleasant,' Sara replied non-committally.

'I was once engaged to her son, Redvers. Small world, isn't it?' Miranda examined the shell-pink varnish on her beautifully shaped nails. 'I daresay you've met him. He's very devoted to his mother and I'm sure he visits her as often as possible.'

'Yes, he called to see her one day last month, soon after I started work at the Crosby.'

'Last month? That's ages ago. Hasn't

he been to see her since?'

'I don't think so — I believe he is working abroad.' Sara had an aversion for telling lies but this statement was only stretching the truth a little. After all, the Scilly Isles could loosely be described as 'abroad' even though they were a part of the British Isles, and she owed it to Caroline to back her up.

Miranda's face fell. 'Oh,' she said, rather disconcerted. 'So the old girl was telling the truth. I rather thought she was leading me up the garden path.'

'Now, why should she do that, I wonder?' Claudia remarked.

'Because she's a possessive old cow,' Miranda snapped. 'She doesn't think I'm the right girl for Redvers. I'm not docile enough. In other words I won't allow myself to be smothered. That's what she tried to do to start with — possess me utterly, but I wasn't having any, so I soon told her where she got off. After that she hadn't got a good word to say for me and she did all she could to cause a rift between us.

Fortunately Redvers was absolutely besotted with me and he didn't take a blind bit of notice. He may still be bound by the silver cord but he's got a will of his own, thank goodness, so the interfering old bag was fighting a lost cause.'

'But she got her way in the end, didn't she?' Claudia pointed out. 'Your engagement was broken off and you married Ronnie Bingham instead.'

'More fool me,' Miranda said with a hollow laugh. 'Incidentally, it wasn't because of Caroline that the engagement was broken off. It was my own doing.' Claudia and Isobel made no comment but, faced by their accusing eyes, she had the grace to look ashamed. 'Yes, I know it was rotten of me,' she admitted, 'but I simply couldn't bear the thought of marrying a cripple. How was I to know Redvers was going to recover? Anyway, I was only twenty and I hadn't much sense in those days. I've grown up since then. Ronnie saw to that,' she added with a hint of bitterness in her voice.

'So you want Redvers back again,' Isobel observed. 'How do you know he'll be willing to play ball? I imagine he was pretty shattered when you gave him back his ring and, from what I know of Redvers Armstrong, he's not the sort of man to forgive and forget.'

'I'm not worried,' Miranda declared. 'I was always able to twist him round my little finger. The annoying thing is he's gone to Canada for six months, so I'll have to wait till he gets back. According to Caroline he's touring around from place to place, with no fixed abode, so I haven't even got an address to write to.'

'There used to be such things as camp followers,' Claudia said nastily.

Miranda glared at her. 'I wish you'd shut up,' she retorted. 'You've been getting at me ever since I arrived. I've got a good mind to pay you out by having a go at Philip though, come to think of it, he's hardly worth the trouble. I'd only have to snap my fingers. Personally I like a challenge,' she continued. 'Someone more like Toby Gregson. He might be fun to have an affair with.'

'He didn't seem particularly interested in you,' Claudia said, with a note of satisfaction in her voice. 'He happens to be keen on Sara.'

'That's the whole point,' Miranda smirked. 'Give me a week — no, less than that — give me five days and I'll have him eating out of my hand.'

Sara was so furious with Miranda for setting her sights on Toby, for no other reason than sheer devilry, that she found her tongue at last.

'I don't see how you'll manage that,' she said, 'considering Toby won't be available. He'll be on the road all next week so you won't get very far with him unless you aim to be a camp follower, as Claudia suggested.'

Claudia clapped her hands. 'Bravo, Sara. That's one in the eye for you, Miranda. You thought Sara was a milksop, didn't you. Well, let me tell you, she isn't, and, in the race for Toby, I'd back Sara against *you* any day.'

'That remains to be seen,' Miranda remarked. 'Certainly a dark horse sometimes wins a race, and that's what you are, aren't you, Sara? A dark horse.'

'I don't know what you mean,' Sara replied, with a catch in her voice.

Miranda fastened her gaze firmly upon her. 'There are a lot of things about you that puzzle me,' she said, 'one of which is this — if you can afford an Elsa Mettam dress, why are you working as a hotel receptionist? Or is it a rude question?'

'You could call it that,' Sara answered, coolly returning her stare. 'I may be only a hotel receptionist but I do have better manners than some people I could name.'

'I was wondering if you have a 'sugar-daddy',' Miranda continued, ignoring the criticism, 'or perhaps a 'sugar-mummy' would be nearer to the truth. Rich women have peculiar whims, and Mrs Armstrong may have plans for you. I warn you, Sara Ravenscroft, don't start getting ideas or it will be the worse for you. I've got first claim on Redvers Armstrong, and I'm pretty handy with a shotgun.'

The gleam in her eye sent cold shivers up and down Sara's spine. This was no idle threat. Miranda was out to get Redvers, come hell or high water, and she would brook no interference to her plans. However, thanks to Caroline's ingenuity, she would have to 'hold her horses' for six months and, meanwhile, it was up to Sara to feign complete innocence.

'I don't know what you're talking about,' she said. 'You must be mad. I hardly know Redvers Armstrong.' 'Then keep it like that,' Miranda snapped and, without waiting for the others, she flounced downstairs.

'You're very quiet,' Toby remarked on the drive home. 'Didn't you enjoy yourself?'

'Miranda spoilt the evening for me,' Sara confessed. 'I found her behaviour intolerable.'

'She's not a nice girl,' Toby agreed. 'I can't think why Isobel invited her — there was never any love lost between them. As for Claudia, she can't stand her.'

They lapsed into a comfortable silence and Sara was grateful to him for being such a pleasant and undemanding companion. Most men would have taken advantage of the lateness of the hour, and of the quiet country road along which they were driving, to park the car on the grass verge in the hope of indulging in a little heavy petting. But not Toby, though she would have been surprised to know how tempted he was to throw caution to the winds. 'Play it cool, man,' he told himself. 'Don't rush in where angels fear to tread.'

'You weren't exactly forthcoming when I suggested earlier on that we should keep in touch,' he said, as he parked the car outside the hotel. 'Was it because you didn't feel you knew me well enough, or is there another man in your life? I wouldn't want to trespass.'

She hesitated. 'Yes, there *is* another man,' she replied. 'I don't know him very well, hardly at all, in fact, and he certainly isn't in love with me but I knew, as soon as I set eyes on him, that as far as *I* was concerned, there would never be anybody else. Does that sound very silly?'

'A fantasy romance?' he queried. 'In real terms you hardly know this man, and yet you say you're in love with him.'

'I know it sounds schoolgirlish and immature,' she admitted, 'but love at first sight does sometimes happen.'

'It's usually reciprocal,' he argued. 'Why hasn't this man followed up the acquaintance or made any effort to see you again?'

'He's abroad,' she said defensively.

'Abroad?' he repeated. 'Not Redvers Armstrong, by any chance?' Hearing her stifled gasp he gave a wry smile. 'I'm sorry,' he apologized, 'I haven't any right to ask. It's just that I know his mother lives at the Crosby and it was only a matter of putting two and two together. I suppose you know he was engaged to Miranda Sutcliffe not so long ago? That was a bad show, giving him back his ring after the plane crash, but it's my belief she's made up her mind to get him back. I gather her marriage to Ronnie Bingham soon turned sour, so she's on the prowl again.'

He hesitated for a moment before continuing. 'A word of warning in your ear. What Miranda wants, she gets, so don't be in too much of a hurry to pin your hopes on Redvers Armstrong. Incidentally, I would hardly call the Scilly Isles 'abroad' but, if the rumour gets around that he's in Canada, it may serve to stall Miranda for the time being, which I imagine is what Mrs Armstrong has in mind. How did I hear about it?' He gave Sara a conspiratorial wink. 'I've been friendly with Redvers for years and I knew about his move to the Scillies, but I didn't consider it any of my business to contradict. If

Redvers's mother says he's in Canada, as far as I'm concerned that's where he is and the longer he stays there the better. No doubt Miranda will find someone to amuse her while he's away and, with a bit of luck she might even get involved with Mark Hardcastle — it would be poetic justice for both of them. Meanwhile, how about *us?* You've made it quite clear that your affections are otherwise engaged but I don't see any reason why we can't date each other. No strings attached, of course. I'll be perfectly happy to pick up any crumbs that drop from your table. So how about it Sara?'

Before she could reply the silence was rudely shattered by the raucous sound of high-powered motor bikes being driven at speed along the seafront. Instinctively she moved closer to him and he immediately put his arm round her, fighting the impulse to caress her slender body. By tilting his head he could lay his cheek against her hair which smelt faintly of jasmine, and he was filled with an overwhelming sense of tenderness. She was more like a flower than any human being he had ever met and he wanted to cherish and protect her. Redvers Armstrong was not worthy of her love and she stood little chance of finding happiness with him.

He had known Redvers since they were boys at school together and he had watched disapprovingly from the side lines when his friend became engaged to Miranda. He had also witnessed the change in Redvers after the plane crash, and he knew that the mental scars caused by the broken engagement went deeper than the physical ones. Disillusion had embittered him and it would be many a long day before he would look kindly on any member of the opposite sex. For Sara the future was bleak by any standard and she would do well to switch her allegiance to someone closer at hand, to a man with hot blood coursing through his veins, whose primitive urges were hers to command. Instinctively he tightened his grip round her waist but, as the noise of the motor bikes receded into the distance, she wriggled out of his grasp.

'Thank heaven for that,' she exclaimed. 'I was afraid they were going to stop.'

'Who *are* they?' he asked. 'Hell's Angels?'

'They call themselves the Mohicans,' she answered. 'They've only appeared during this last week but they're real troublemakers.'

'The *Mohicans?*' he repeated. 'What on earth do they think they're up to?'

'They're dressed as Red Indians,' she told him, 'only they ride motor bikes instead of horses. They've got all the gear — feather headdresses, leather jerkins, moccasins, bows and arrows — the lot. Must have cost them a bomb.'

'The new cult?' he hazarded. 'Teenagers have always got to have something. Teddy boys, the flower people, punk rockers, hell's angels . . . and now the Mohicans. It's a form of rebellion, I suppose. They'll grow out of it eventually and, by and large, they're pretty harmless.'

'The Mohicans aren't,' she shuddered. 'The other night they held a pow-wow on the beach just opposite the hotel. I can't describe it. It was somehow . . . menacing. Miss Benson made light of it but I could see she was concerned.'

'Why didn't she report them to the police?'

'There wasn't much point. It's not as if they were causing a breach of the peace.'

'A pow-wow on the beach, opposite the hotel?' he repeated thoughtfully. 'They must have chosen their pitch for a definite purpose. Has anyone got a grudge against Miss Benson?'

'That's the worrying thing about it,' Sara replied. 'She dismissed a waiter a week or two ago for stealing and she thinks she recognized him as one of the

Mohicans, though it's a bit difficult to tell under all that warpaint. I really must go, Toby, or my name will be mud with the night porter, so I'll say good-night and thanks for the lift.'

'My pleasure,' he replied, and he got out of his side of the car and came round to open the passenger door for her. 'I'll phone you some time before Friday and we'll try to fix a date for next week-end. How soon will you know when you'll be off duty?'

'Except for my days off, which are Mondays and Thursdays, my hours are rather elastic,' she told him, 'but Miss Benson is super to work for and we fit in with each other very well.'

'I'll see you next Friday, then?'

'Hopefully — yes,' she answered, glad to be able to accept his invitation with a clear conscience. She had told him the truth about her feelings for Redvers so he couldn't turn round and accuse her of leading him up the garden path. Fortunately he seemed content with the idea of having a platonic friendship with her and, if he kept it that way, there was no reason why they shouldn't have a good time together.

5

The night porter was still bright-eyed and bushy-tailed, having only come on duty a couple of hours ago. 'Had a good time, Miss?' he asked, thinking, not for the first time, what a 'smasher' she was. She was nice, too, which was something you couldn't say about some of the girls nowadays who seemed to think about nothing except dolling themselves up and going off for a night on the tiles. Bill Watkins was one of the old school, nearer seventy than sixty, and he hadn't moved with the times. 'Glad to see you got back safely,' he continued. 'It's not nice being out after dark, what with those crazy Mohicans on the rampage. Fair sick of them, I am, kicking up a row night after night. They ought to be clapped in irons. Don't know why they don't bring back the birch. That'd teach them a thing or two, noisy young devils.'

'You were young once, Bill,' she reminded him. 'I daresay you got up to plenty of mischief when you were in your prime.'

'Mischief — yes,' he agreed, 'but not downright nastiness. Mark my words, we haven't heard the last of those Mohicans.'

'Oh well,' she said, half jokingly, 'as long as they don't start throwing flaming arrows and setting people's property on fire.'

'Wouldn't put it past them,' he grumbled. 'Well, goodnight, Miss. I mustn't keep you talking or you'll miss your beauty sleep.'

'Good-night, Bill.' She blew him a kiss. 'I hope the Mohicans don't come back and scalp you.'

'They'd better not try it,' he scowled, flexing his muscles. 'There's plenty of life in the old dog yet.'

Before going upstairs Sara paused for a moment outside Caroline's bedroom but there was no light showing under the door, so perhaps she had been mistaken in thinking she had seen the curtains twitch. In any case it was hardly likely that the older woman would wait up till well past midnight in order to satisfy herself that her protégée had come safely home. Sara would be able to tell her all about the dinner party in the morning when she took in her breakfast tray, and no doubt she would be interested to hear that Miranda had been one of the guests.

In fact, she was even more interested than Sara had expected her to be. Interested, and a little concerned lest Sara might have inadvertently let the cat out of the bag with regard to Redvers's present wherabouts.

'I was very careful,' Sara assured her. 'She managed to winkle out of me that I work at the Crosby and, after that, she kept on and on about you and Redvers, how well I know you, and did Redvers visit very often and all that sort of thing. I was very vague and just said I believed he was working abroad, which seemed to satisfy her. She admitted she had wondered whether you were telling her the truth about him going to Canada for six months, but I'm happy to say she no longer has any doubts.'

'Splendid,' Caroline beamed. 'So that takes care of Miranda for the time being. Now you've met her I'm sure you agree with me that she's a most obnoxious girl.'

'I must say I didn't take to her,' Sara replied, 'but she seems to appeal to the opposite sex.'

Caroline nodded. 'To their baser instincts — yes,' she agreed. 'But I shudder to think how unhappy Redvers would be if he married her.'

'Do you really think he'd take her back after the way she treated him?' Sara asked.

'I'm certain he would,' Caroline answered, 'which is why I'll move heaven and earth to keep them apart.' Uttering a small sigh she put her hand to her head. 'I find this reappearance of

Miranda extremely worrying,' she continued. 'I hardly slept a wink last night and those wretched Mohicans didn't help. I heard them come back again at about two o'clock and they stopped outside the hotel and did a war dance. I don't know what Brighton's coming to. It never used to be like this, but the whole world is changing, and not for the better. I wonder if things are different in the Scilly Isles. Redvers finds the life there very pleasant and I'm quite tempted to go and see for myself.'

'Why don't you?' Sara asked. 'A holiday would do you good.'

'Perhaps I will, but I wouldn't like to undertake the journey alone.'

'Surely Redvers would come and fetch you?'

'That's the problem,' Caroline told her. 'I have an aversion to the sea — the moment I set foot on a boat I'm seasick, even on the calmest day, and Redvers has this phobia about flying. So you see, it's a stalemate as far as my son and I are concerned. But never fear — if I *do* decide to go, I'll think of some way out of the difficulty.' She gave a dismissive nod and, as Sara went out of the room, her glance rested thoughtfully on the girl's retreating back. Of course, Sara wasn't due for a holiday, at any rate until the end of the season, but it would be nice if she could persuade her to go with her. It would give Redvers the opportunity of getting to know her better because these brief visits, spaced so far apart, were not very productive.

The following morning she was delighted to receive an unexpected letter from him. He and his partner were looking for a new secretary because their present 'Man Friday' was taking early retirement due to ill health. 'There is no shortage of girl typists on the island,' he wrote, 'but male secretaries are at a premium and we both prefer the idea of a man working for us. Would you get in touch with that agency in Hove and interview the most likely candidates? Then, on my next visit, I could make the final choice.'

Immediately she had finished reading the letter Caroline began to make plans. This request of Redvers's was most fortuitous and it would need only a little manoeuvring on her part to get that sweet girl, Sara Ravenscroft, established in the Scilly Isles as his secretary. She dismissed as unimportant the fact that her son and his partner had specifically asked for a male secretary, nor did she mention this to Sara when she told her what she had in mind.

'I have wonderful news for you, my dear,' she said, 'Redvers has asked me to find a secretary for him and I immediately thought of you. It's a splendid opportunity. The salary is good and you will live as one of the family in the house Redvers shares with his partner, so you will have no problems moneywise. The job is yours for the taking and you can start as soon as you like.' She favoured Sara with a beaming smile. 'It will solve my own difficulty at the same time because we can keep each other company on the journey. Yes, I have decided to go there for a holiday,' she continued. 'You have no objection to flying, I hope? All your travelling expenses will be paid, of course.'

Sara was completely taken aback and she stared at Caroline in stunned dismay. If only she could accept such a fabulous offer, how blissful it would be, but she had promised to stay with Evelyn, at any rate till the end of the season and, however tempting the prospect, she couldn't possibly go back on her word, especially as a notification from the hospital had come through the post that very morning, informing Miss Benson there had been a cancellation and that her long awaited operation had been scheduled for Wednesday.

'How kind of you to suggest it,' she said, 'but I'm afraid I can't possibly accept. I have a commitment here and I couldn't leave at the drop of a hat.'

'What absolute rubbish! Nobody's indispensable,' Caroline thundered. 'If you don't accept my offer I shall take it as a personal insult.'

Sara was nearly in tears. Having to turn her back on such a wonderful opportunity was bad enough but the idea of having Caroline as an enemy instead of a friend was almost insupportable. Without her assistance she would never get to know Redvers better and all her romantic dreams would turn to dust. 'Please don't be angry,' she begged. 'It's a matter of integrity. I promised Miss Benson I would stay and I couldn't live with myself if I broke my word.'

Seeing she was genuinely distressed, Caroline simmered down but her heightened colour betrayed the fact that she was still furious. It was ludicrous that her plans should be thwarted by Sara's misguided sense of loyalty, though she couldn't help feeling a sneaking admiration for the girl's courage.

'Very well, Sara,' she said in a gentler tone of voice, 'if you feel like that it's no good arguing with you about it. We'll leave it for the time being but, if we put our minds to it, perhaps we can work out a solution that will please everybody.'

On this optimistic note she went back to her bedroom and penned a hurried note to Redvers, telling him she had every hope of finding a suitable secretary for him in the near future. 'And now to work on Miss Benson's good nature,' she said briskly to herself when she returned from posting her letter. 'She's very fond of Sara and I'm sure she won't stand in her way. After all, hotel receptionists are two a penny and it's not as if Sara's a fixture.'

But Evelyn was nowhere to be found. On receiving her notification from the hospital she had rushed out to have a perm and she planned to take the rest of the day off to do some shopping and to brief the friend who had promised to act as a stand-in during her enforced absence.

When she learnt what was happening even Caroline had to admit it was hardly the best time for Sara to leave but, with any luck, Evelyn would only be in hospital for a few days and, all being well, she would have convalesced sufficiently by the middle of June to take up the reins again.

Evelyn's friend, Charmaine Lessimore, turned out to be more of a figurehead than a pillar of strength. Consequently Sara had to work twice as hard as usual and, when Toby phoned during the week, anxious to make a date with Sara for the week-end, she was obliged to tell him she wouldn't be free.

'Miss Benson's in hospital,' she explained, 'and all my off duty has gone by the board.'

'Surely you can get off for an hour or two? he grumbled.

'I don't like leaving the hotel,' she replied, 'in case anything crops up. Miss

Benson's friend is officially in charge but she's decorative rather than useful.'

'I know the type,' he said glumly. 'Look, why can't I drop in at the hotel on Friday evening, and we can sit in the bar and have a drink and a chat? You'd still be on hand in case you were needed, but it would give you a chance to relax.'

'Super,' she agreed, genuinely pleased at the idea of seeing him again. 'Shall we say nine o'clock? Things should have eased off by then.'

'Any more trouble with the Mohicans?' he asked.

'Not a breath or a whisper,' she replied, keeping her fingers crossed. 'I think the police must have scared them off, at any rate for the time being. See you on Friday then.' She rang off as the pips sounded and turned to attend to one of the guests who informed her that the hot tap in her wash basin was leaking, and could it please be attended to as soon as possible.

'I don't want to be a nuisance, dear,'

she said apologetically, 'but, if it drips all night, I won't be able to get a wink of sleep.'

'I can't possibly get hold of a plumber at eight o'clock in the evening,' Sara thought distractedly. 'It will have to wait till Bill comes on duty at ten. Luckily he seems to be able to turn his hand to anything.'

Inevitably, as the week progressed, more and more problems cropped up and by Friday evening, when she walked into the bar with Toby, Sara felt completely drained. 'You look a bit under the weather,' he remarked, glancing at her with some concern as she sipped her gin and tonic.

'It's been a hectic week,' she admitted, 'but I'm glad to say Miss Benson's making a good recovery.'

'She was lucky she had you to fall back on,' he commented, 'but don't overdo it, Sara. It isn't worth it. Charmaine is the one who'll get all the credit.' He nodded in the direction of Miss Lessimore who was doing her hostess act at the far end of the lounge. 'You know the proverb about the willing horse.'

'And the one about the last straw breaking the camel's back?' Sara laughed, making an effort to sparkle. 'I've still a long way to go before that happens. As long as the Mohicans keep away, I can cope.'

'You're really worried about them, aren't you?' he said.

A shadow crossed her face. 'I keep thinking they may come back,' she answered. 'I dreamed about them last night, one of those horrible vivid dreams where everything takes place in slow motion. You're trying to run but your legs are as heavy as lead and you don't make any progress. I was just going to be scalped when I woke up.'

'Poor Sara.' He touched her cheek briefly with the back of his hand, a tender gesture which made the tears spring to her eyes.

'Oh, Toby,' she whispered. 'What a comfort you are.'

Caroline, who had been watching them from the vantage point of her favourite chair, stifled an exclamation of dismay. If Toby was getting ideas it would be as well to nip them in the bud.

Getting up from her chair she approached the bar with elaborate casualness and ordered a scotch on the rocks. 'Why!' she exclaimed in pretended surprise. 'If it isn't Toby Gregson! Sara, my dear, how nice to see you relaxing for a change. You've been working far too hard all the week. May I join you?' she added and, without waiting for a reply, she ensconced herself firmly in the chair next to Sara's, where she remained, as immovable as a stone buddha, until Toby said, in desperation, that it was time for him to go.

'I'll walk with you to the car,' Sara offered, jumping up with alacrity. She, too, had found Caroline's insensitivity rather trying, though not to the same extent as Toby who had been looking forward all the week to getting Sara to himself.

'I'll come too,' Caroline insisted, linking her arm in Sara's. 'It's a lovely evening for a walk and, after Toby's gone, we can stroll along the seafront. A breath of air will do you good.'

'I'll phone you,' Toby said, *sotto voce* to Sara as he got into his car. 'I quite thought chaperones had gone out of fashion, but Mrs Armstrong evidently belongs to the old school.' He frowned at Caroline who was standing almost within earshot, nonchalantly studying the stars. 'We'll have to think of some other way of meeting,' he continued. 'It's a pity you haven't got a downstair bedroom — I haven't had much practice in abseiling.'

'Don't you dare try it,' she said, stifling a giggle at the though of Toby climbing up to her 'crow's nest' perched high under the eaves.

'I'll find a way, even if it means borrowing a fireman's ladder,' he joked and, giving her a meaningful look, he drove off, little dreaming that this was exactly what he would have to do before many hours had passed.

It was nearly two o'clock in the morning when Sara awoke to the smell of burning. She lay for a moment, collecting her senses and, when she realized what was happening, she was out of bed in a flash. Going over to the window she looked out onto a terrifying scene. The whole hotel was ablaze, with flames leaping out of every downstair window, and, even as she watched, she saw three of the Mohicans, naked to the waist and covered with warpaint, run across the lawn to shoot more flaming arrows into the inferno.

She realized the din had been going on for some time and she must have been sleeping like a log not to have heard it. Hastily grabbing a dressing-gown she opened her bedroom door, with one thought in her mind — to escape before the blaze engulfed the upstair landing. But she was already too late. A great pall of smoke greeted her, sending her coughing and choking back to the comparative safety of her bedroom. Fortunately she had the good sense to slam the door shut before flinging open the window, and she stood there, shouting for help with all the power of her lungs.

By now the fire engine had arrived and the Mohicans had slipped stealthily away into the darkness. Tonight they had come on foot so there had been no sound of approaching motor bikes to give them away. By the time the hue and cry was out they would be safely back in bed and no doubt they would swear they had never left their houses.

After what seemed an eternity Sara saw Toby racing round the side of the hotel, followed by Caroline and Charmaine. They stood beneath her bedroom window, their upturned faces glowing with an unearthly light as the reflection of the flames danced across them, and Toby was gesticulating with both arms and imploring her not to jump. It was like a scene from an old-fashioned melodrama but terribly, dreadfully real.

Sara was almost at her last gasp when two firemen appeared with an extending ladder, but it was Toby who thrust the men aside and insisted on rescuing her himself. His calm voice and masterly handling of the situation prevented Sara from panicking and soon she was safely on *terra firma*.

'My dear Sara,' cried Caroline, tears of relief coursing down her cheeks. 'Thank God you're all right.'

'I'm taking you home with me,' Toby said in a voice that brooked no argument and, bearing her in his arms, he carried her through the throng of gaping sightseers to his car, which he had parked on the seafront, well out of the danger zone.

'I hadn't gone to bed when the fire started,' he explained, 'so I came along to investigate. Of course I didn't know it was the Crosby till I got here and I nearly had a heart attack when Mrs Armstrong told me you were trapped at the top of the house. Heaven knows how the flames got a hold so quickly. I presume there were fire doors and adequate precautions?'

'Yes, of course,' she answered in a husky whisper, 'but it was those dreadful Mohicans. You don't expect flaming arrows to be thrown in this day and age.'

He whistled incredulously. 'So that's what Mrs Armstrong meant when she said poor old Bill Watkins had been scalped. She didn't mean it literally, of course, because I saw him wandering around with a full head of hair, but he's got a whopping great bruise on his temple, so I suppose the Mohicans knocked him out before they set fire to the place. One thing's certain. This can't be dismissed as a teenage prank. Those boys are in dead trouble and I imagine the sacked waiter was at the bottom of it.'

Lying her tenderly on the back seat of the car, he covered her with a rug and she was in a semi-conscious state when they arrived at his parents' home. Afterwards she had only a vague memory of being undressed by Mrs Gregson and put in a warm bath, and she was so exhausted from her unnerving experience that she was fast asleep almost before getting into bed. Toby insisted on spending the rest of the night in the same room and, when she woke the next morning, the sun was shining onto the recumbent form of her knight errant.

Studying him as he slept, she thought what a nice face he had. Here was a man one could be comfortable with, for he would never be moody, bad-tempered or unreasonable. Life with him would pursue a pleasant, unchequered course, never plumbing the depths, nor reaching the stars. Completely satisfactory in its own way. Nevertheless, the thought of leading such an ordered existence left her singularly unmoved.

A vision of Redvers swam before her eyes, his countenance dark, passionate and brooding, and a shiver of ecstasy ran up and down her spine. She could feel his mouth on hers, bruising her lips and causing a pain so exquisite it was not torture but bliss. This was the man she loved with every fibre of her being and no other could take his place. She was his for better, for worse, in sickness and in health, and she was as committed to him as if she had already taken her marriage vows.

When would she see him again, she wondered. What hope had she got of ever meeting up with him, now that the hotel where his mother lived lay in smouldering ruins? Caroline would move on to another hotel, or else go and settle in the Scilly Isles, and Sara would have to look around for another job. All contact with Redvers would be lost and the tiny bud of romance which she had been nurturing in her heart would wilt and fade before ever reaching maturity.

Despair swept over her but she suddenly saw a ray of hope. Redvers had asked his mother to find a secretary for him and Caroline had offered her the job, which she had had to turn down because she had promised Evelyn not to leave her in the lurch. The situation had now changed dramatically and she was no longer bound by that promise, but free to go to the Scilly Isles as soon as the necessary arrangements could be made. Her heart beat faster and she quivered with joy at the prospect of meeting Redvers again, of living in the same house with him and seeing him every day.

Meanwhile there were many problems to be faced but, as it turned out, everything was made easy for her. Mrs Gregson lent her some clothes to wear and insisted she should stay with them until she had decided what she was going to do. Then Caroline telephoned to say she had managed to salvage most of her own possessions and that Charmaine had offered her temporary accommodation in her flat. Despite the inconvenience and upset caused by the fire, she sounded remarkably cheerful and she promised to take Sara shopping with her on Monday morning. She planned to travel to the Scilly Isles later in the week and she took it for granted her protégée would go with her.

'Everything has turned out for the best,' she said with undisguised satisfaction. 'You'll be able to accept that secretarial post after all. I phoned Redvers and suggested he should book me in at a hotel or guest house, but the season is in full swing and the island is chock-a-block with tourists, so we shall both be staying in the house Redvers shares with his partner. I gather there is only one spare bedroom so you will be accommodated in Mr Willis's quarters. The poor man has had a heart attack and is in hospital so he won't be around to show you the ropes, but I'm sure you haven't a thing to worry about. You'll settle into the routine in no time at all.'

Sara was not so sure. She knew little or nothing about agricultural affairs, and the prospect of taking over without

Mr Willis's help rather daunted her. However, she had made a success of being a hotel receptionist despite her lack of experience and she could only hope that her luck would hold. Redvers was not the type to suffer fools gladly and if she did not give complete satisfaction, he would have no hesitation in giving her the sack.

The next few days were extremely hectic but Toby was a tower of strength. In order to be of as much assistance as possible he took the week off work and he put himself entirely at Sara's disposal, much to the annoyance of Caroline, who made no attempt to hide the way she felt about him. Sara was pulled in both directions and keeping peace between the two antagonists required all her resources of tact and diplomacy.

Fortunately for Caroline she was in a far stronger position than Toby and, when she and Sara got into the plane for the start of the first leg of their journey, she had the satisfaction of knowing that Redvers's rival was, to all intents and purposes, out of the running. The Scilly Isles were sufficiently far away to prevent him dropping in for an hour or two and, although absence is said to make the heart grow fonder, it does not always work out like that.

'It's lucky we're going so far away,' Caroline decided, 'and none too soon by the look of things. That young man is getting far too keen on Sara for my peace of mind.'

Fastening her seat belt preparatory to take off, she was relieved to see that Sara did not even turn her head for one last look at the man who had served her so devotedly. All her thoughts were concentrated on what lay ahead, on her new job, her new life — and on Redvers and, as they became airborne, she was so anxious to reach her journey's end that her impatient heart outdistanced the plane, and she sat beside Caroline, like a puppet on a string, going through all the motions expected of her, but almost in a trance. Afterwards she had no recollection of the journey. It seemed to her that one moment she was getting on a plane at Heathrow and the next she was alighting from a helicopter at St Mary's Airport and eagerly looking out for Redvers's tall figure.

But it was not Redvers who met them. It was his partner, Guy Sheridan. He told Caroline that Redvers had been unable to spare the time to come to the airport but, although this was a perfectly valid explanation, Sara sensed there was more to it than that. She was also certain that Guy looked extremely taken aback, and none too pleased, when Caroline introduced her as the new secretary. He shook hands civilly enough but Sara's mood of euphoria vanished abruptly.

For some unexplained reason her presence was an embarrassment and, however hard Guy tried to disguise the fact, it was plain that neither he nor Redvers wanted her on the island.

6

Caroline did not seem to be aware of anything amiss but Sara had noticed before that Redvers's mother had a singular talent for ignoring things that were not to her liking. She knew that she herself was oversensitive, so she may have been mistaken in thinking that Guy's welcome had been lacking in warmth. At any rate one mystery was quickly cleared up and, to her great relief, she found she had misconstrued the reason for Redvers's non-appearance at the airport. The simple truth was that he was still suffering from his phobia and, whenever possible, he avoided coming within earshot of air traffic. Living as he did in the north of the island, he was spared the trauma of low-flying aircraft continually passing overhead but, nonetheless, the menace was there and he was sometimes caught unawares by the sound of a plane or helicopter flying sightseers from the mainland around the Isles on a pleasure trip.

Despite the passage of time, his obsessive fear showed no sign of abating and, although he was perfectly happy to drive into Hugh Town and deliver their produce for export via the *Scillonian*, he invariably left it to Guy when an urgent order was being transported by air. Guy knew better than to argue with him and, if he believed that Redvers would be wise to face up to his fear, he kept his opinion to himself.

'We've had a good year,' he remarked as he put Caroline's and Sara's luggage into the estate car. 'Business has been booming ever since Redvers came into partnership with me. As you probably know I inherited the market garden from my uncle and I optimistically thought I could run it at a profit, but it was already in pretty poor shape and I hadn't the know-how — or the resources — to turn it into a paying concern. I wouldn't have lasted a month if it hadn't been for good old Willis's assistance. He was my uncle's secretary and he knows the business from A to Z, but he lacks vision and neither of us realized how important it is to move with the times. To cut a long story short we muddled along in the same old way until we stood on the brink of disaster. That was when Redvers stepped in. You can take it from me Mrs Armstrong, that son of yours is a genius.'

Caroline preened herself. 'Redvers has always been outstanding,' she agreed. 'He makes a success of everything he puts his mind to and, if it hadn't been for that dreadful plane crash, I'm convinced he would have made his mark as an architect. I dreamed of him becoming a second Edwin Lutyens but it was not to be.' She uttered a nostalgic sigh. 'However, you can't keep a good man down and he appears to have adapted very well to his change of venue.'

'To my benefit,' Guy said with a cheerful grin. He seemed to have recovered from his shock at seeing Sara but, every now and then, he gave her a puzzled glance, and she had a feeling he was sizing her up. She hoped that, whatever it was that was worrying him would soon be satisfactorily resolved because they would be living in the same house and working in close association with each other, so a friendly relation-ship was essential. Through no known fault of her own she appeared to have started off on the wrong foot and she was puzzled, and more than a little upset, by his hostile attitude.

Would Redvers react in the same way, she wondered. Surely Caroline had told him that Sara Ravenscroft and the new secretary were one and the same person? Even if she hadn't done so, it wouldn't explain the expression of stunned surprise on Guy's face when they were introduced. There was some mystery here and the sooner it was cleared up the better.

The drive along the rather narrow road leading from the airport temporarily took her mind off the problem and she looked eagerly out of the window. June is proverbially the month of roses but never had she seen flowers in such abundance. Of every sort and colour, they crowded together in cottage gardens, spilled from window boxes, stone troughs and wooden containers, and filled the air with perfume. Sara sat entranced, silently assimilating the sights and sounds of this perfect summer's day, while the two in the front seat exchanged desultory chat, seeming not to notice the beauty of their surroundings.

When they arrived at their destination Guy unloaded their suitcases and showed them to their rooms, Caroline's at the front of the house and Sara's along the passage, facing the greenhouse field. 'I'll see if I can find Redvers,' he said and, without more ado, he took his departure, leaving Sara to wonder why she had been put in a room so essentially masculine.

It was spotlessly clean and everything had been meticulously polished, possibly by Guy's wife, Sara surmised, but in that case why was she not here to greet them? Sara had taken it for granted that Redvers's partner was married but she may well have been mistaken. Presumably the housework and cooking were done by a daily woman and, if this was the case, Sara and Caroline had descended on an all-male household and, judging by the fact that nothing had been changed since Mr Willis's departure, it seemed likely that a male secretary had been expected to take his place.

But surely Caroline had told Redvers she had offered Sara the job? Surely she hadn't let him believe the new secretary was a man? If she had deliberately kept them in the dark this would account for Guy's look of surprise when he saw her, and Sara trembled to think what Redvers would say when he discovered that his mother had deceived him. Naturally he would jump to the conclusion that Sara had been in cahoots with Caroline, and he would look upon her as a conniving female.

Going over to the window she could see Guy crossing the field with quick, purposeful strides. He went into one of the greenhouses and a few minutes later reappeared with Redvers. They were deep in conversation and Sara drew hurriedly back from the window, for fear of being seen.

Presently she heard Caroline's door open and shut and the sound of her footsteps as she went down the stairs. Discretion being the better part of valour, Sara stayed where she was, hoping that Redvers's mother would bear the brunt of his anger, and that he would have cooled down by the time his new secretary made her appearance.

Being a prudent man Guy, also, made himself scarce, so mother and son had a head-on confrontation, with no audience.

'What's this I hear about you bringing Sara Ravenscroft with you?' Redvers asked without preamble. 'I specifically stated we wanted a male secretary.'

'But *darling*,' Caroline protested, all wide-eyed innocence, 'I didn't think it was all that important. What difference can it make whether your secretary is male or female as long as she gives satisfaction?'

'This is an all-male household,' Redvers told her, his voice charged with exasperation. 'It would be different if Guy was married but how do you think it's going to look, having a girl living here? A *ménage a trois* may be tolerated in England but, in the Scillies, we still bow to convention.'

'But *I* shall be here as her chaperone,' Caroline pointed out.

'For how long?' he barked. 'By the end of a week you'll be bored to tears. We're quite isolated here and there's nothing to do in the way of amusements unless you like rock-scrambling or bird-watching. What I have in mind for you is a house in Hugh Town. I've already got a list from the estate agents.' He indicated a pile of leaflets on the table. 'We would be close enough to see each other as often as we like but we wouldn't be living in each other's pockets.'

'I'm sure I shall be quite happy here for the time being,' Caroline replied. 'In any case it always takes time to buy a property and I wouldn't want to do anything in a hurry. If I like the life I may decide to settle here permanently, if not I can always return to Brighton.'

'What about Sara?' he reminded her. 'I trust she's not hoping to dig herself in. She must be made to understand this will only be a temporary job. I have no intention of employing a woman secretary on a permanent basis.'

'She may well find something else before the end of the season,' Caroline remarked cryptically. 'Don't be angry, Redvers. Once you get to know Sara better you'll get along like a house on fire. Which reminds me — the poor girl lost everything in that disastrous blaze at the hotel. Her job, her possessions — almost her life.'

'I was sorry about that,' he allowed, 'but it doesn't excuse the way in which she's cashing in on your good nature. I suppose it was she who suggested coming to the Scilly Isles with you, and no doubt she persuaded you to conveniently forget I asked for a male secretary. Let me tell you, Mother, I don't like being taken for a ride.'

Caroline rushed to Sara's defence, assuring Redvers that the girl had been completely innocent of any connivance, but he clearly did not believe her and, when Sara finally made her appearance, his manner was frosty to the extreme.

She had waited ten minutes — the longest ten minutes in her life — before coming downstairs, and her nerves were at screaming point as she hesitated outside the half open door. To meet Redvers again, to talk to him, what a joyful occasion it would have been had it not been marred by this wretched misunderstanding.

As she came into the room their eyes met and, for a long moment, neither of them spoke. Then he gave her a cool nod. 'I'm sure you realize your presence here is somewhat embarrassing,' he remarked. 'I specifically asked my mother to engage a male secretary but my wishes have been ignored and we find ourselves in an impasse. If it was left to me I would ask you to take the next flight back to England but my mother has interceded on your behalf. She says you are without a job and practically destitute, so I can hardly turn you out at a moment's notice. The only suggestion I can make is that you stay here while my mother is still in residence, and that you take over Mr Willis's job on a temporary basis, 'temporary' being the operative word. That must be made quite clear from the start.'

Sara supposed he was being kind but

her hackles rose at the arrogant way in which he put forward his proposal. However, she had no alternative but to eat humble pie and, with heightened colour and trembling lip, she accepted his offer. 'I hope I shall give satisfaction, *sir*,' she said, giving sufficient stress to the word to bring a look of discomfiture to his face. 'If you will show me where Mr Willis's office is I would like to familiarize myself with the agenda straightaway.'

'For heaven's sake!' he exclaimed irritably. 'There's no need for that. Another twelve hours isn't going to make any difference to the muddle we're in. Mr Willis had a heart attack last week and he's still in hospital, so the office is in a hell of a mess.' He ran a hand distractedly through his hair in a gesture Sara found oddly appealing. 'Guy and I haven't been able to cope with the paperwork as well as everything else, so we've had to let things slide. I only hope you're as efficient as my mother says you are, otherwise we shall be in dead trouble.' He turned to Caroline. 'I'm afraid I can't stop and entertain you,' he apologized, 'but I have work to do. By the way, supper is at half past six. Mrs Foster comes mornings and evenings to cook and clean for us, and she should be here shortly.'

He took himself off without a second glance in Sara's direction and she found she was trembling from head to foot. Caroline, on the other hand, was completely self-possessed. 'That's one hurdle less to cross,' she announced with satisfaction. 'It wasn't too bad, was it?'

'He was very angry,' Sara said in a husky whisper.

Caroline nodded. 'A little put out, shall we say? Redvers never did like being crossed, but he'll get over it. I'm sure we did the right thing in ignoring his stupid whim about having a male secretary.'

'I knew nothing about it,' Sara said reproachfully. 'You should have told me. As it is I'm being made to feel I'm here under false pretences. I'm sure Redvers will never forgive me.'

'Nonsense!' Caroline exclaimed. 'When he's had time to mull it over he'll realize what a godsend you are. On his own admission he and Guy are in a terrible pickle and, once you've sorted everything out, they'll be so grateful they'll want you to stay on.'

'I hope so,' Sara sighed, 'but I don't feel very self-confident. It wouldn't be so bad if Mr Willis was around to show me the ropes but I shall be strictly on my own and I've no idea what will be expected of me.'

'Think what a success you made of being a hotel receptionist,' Caroline said encouragingly. 'You'd had no previous experience of that sort of work but in no time at all you became Miss Benson's right-hand man. Now, I suggest we go for a bit of a stroll before supper and get our bearings. I believe we're quite near a golf course and I expect there's a club we can join.'

'I've never played,' Sara confessed. 'In any case, I won't have much spare time for recreation.'

'I won't allow Redvers to treat you like a slave,' Caroline replied. 'One of the reasons I brought you here was to be a companion to me and I shall insist you're given adequate time off.'

They linked arms and, as they walked along the highways and byways, Sara became more relaxed, and she quickly got the 'feel' of the island. The vistas were enchanting, whether heathland or open sea, and she could hardly resist scrambling down the rocks onto the sandy shore to paddle her toes in the crystal clear water.

They returned to the house to find the admirable Mrs Foster had been busy during their absence, and they sat down to a hearty meal of home-made steak and kidney pie, served with freshly picked vegetables. This was followed by gooseberry crumble with clotted cream, and Caroline laughingly remarked that, if this was a sample of their daily fare, she would have to watch her figure.

Sara was very quiet, well aware that Redvers was still exceedingly angry, not only with his mother but also with her. They had played a trick on him which he would not easily forgive, and he responded to Caroline's questions with a modicum of politeness, while at the same time ignoring Sara completely. Occasionally Guy took pity on her and tried to draw her into the conversation, but it was Caroline who did most of the talking, and she waffled on like a stream in full spate, skilfully ensuring there were no awkward silences.

As soon as the meal was over Sara pleaded a headache and retired to her bedroom, unable to stand the strain any longer. She had built such high hopes on this trip to the Scillies but now she felt humiliated and dejected, and it was all Caroline's fault for being so foolish as to ignore her son's wishes. Sara did not blame Redvers for being annoyed, but it was unreasonable of him to take it out on her when she was completely innocent, and she made up her mind to exonerate herself at the earliest opportunity.

This opportunity came sooner than she expected, though unfortunately it was Guy and not Redvers to whom she told her tale of woe. A short rest on the bed had quickly cured her headache and she did not relish the prospect of spending the rest of the evening in her room, so she tiptoed downstairs, intending to go for a solitary walk and to return before the household retired for the night.

There was still an hour of daylight left and the air was soft and balmy, faintly perfumed with the scent of a million flowers. Earlier in the evening she had walked with Caroline as far as Watermill Cove but now she took the path leading in the opposite direction. In his letters Redvers had often described the glory of the sunsets and she wanted to see for herself the magical sight of a 'golden sun reflected in a golden sea.'

She was to see this incredible scene repeated many times in the future and she was always to experience the same sense of awe as on this first occasion. 'Beautiful beyond belief' were the words Redvers had used to describe it and she longed to share her joy with him, to stand beside him and watch in wonder as the golden sun sank below the horizon.

It could have been so, had she come to the island at his invitation, instead of against his wishes, but they were back to square one and he was treating her with the same hostility he had shown when Caroline had invited her to go to Abbotsfield with them. Admittedly he had become more friendly as the day wore on but he was clearly extremely annoyed that she had been foisted on him for a second time. He probably believed she had sucked up to Caroline and wangled the invitation on both occasions, and he may have got the feeling he was being chased. Sara's cheeks burned at the very thought because, even in these days of woman's lib, it is the man's prerogative to make the running — especially if that man is over thirty — and woe betide the girl who steps out of line.

Busy with her thoughts she did not hear Guy's footsteps on the soft, spongy turf. 'There you are,' he said, speaking quietly so as not to make her jump. 'Mrs Armstrong was worried when she found you weren't in your room and she asked me to come and look for you. She was afraid you may have got lost.'

Sara detected a slight hesitation before the word 'me' and she guessed Caroline had asked Redvers first and that he had delegated the unsavoury task to his partner.

'I'm sorry,' she apologized. 'I didn't realize it was so late. How did you know where to find me?'

'Redvers saw you leaving the house and noticed you were walking in this direction. I expect you wanted to see the sunset. It's one of our tourist attractions,' he added with a smile.

'I'm not a tourist,' she reminded him. 'I've come here to work. Look, Guy, I seem to have got off on the wrong foot but I honestly didn't know you and Redvers wanted a male secretary. Caroline offered me the job several weeks ago but I turned it down because I'd only recently started working at the hotel and I could hardly leave Miss Benson in the lurch at the height of the season. After the fire Caroline said you were still not suited and she made out that Redvers would be delighted to have me, so I naturally agreed to come, but I would never have done so if I'd known the set-up. I can see what an embarrassing situation it is for both of you but it's none of my doing and it's very unkind of Redvers to take it out on me.' Her voice broke in a sob and Guy made a clumsy effort to comfort her, putting his arm round her and letting her cry against his shoulder.

Presently she cheered up. 'Sorry about that,' she said, giving a final sniff and managing a watery smile. 'I'm not usually such a wet but the last few days have been pretty hectic, and to find I'm not wanted here was the last straw.'

'*I* want you,' he said unexpectedly. 'I think you'll prove to be the best thing that has happened to us for a long time.'

Sara gave his arm a squeeze. 'It's nice of you to say so,' she replied. 'Tomorrow will be the testing day and I only hope I'll justify your faith in me.'

'I'm sure you will,' he answered, doing his best to boost her morale. She was a nice little person and he had taken quite a fancy to her. Strictly in an avuncular way, of course, because she was much younger than he was. Just right for Redvers, though, and he hoped something would come of it. Theirs had been an all-male household for too long and, although he himself was a born bachelor, Redvers certainly was not. At times Guy suspected his partner still had a yen for the girl who had jilted him. Perhaps he even hoped for a reconciliation, and this might account for the fact that he pointedly ignored the pretty young maidens of Hugh Town who set their caps at him.

Guy had never actually met Miranda but, from the little Redvers had told him, he had formed the opinion that she was definitely not a nice girl and that his partner was better off without her. 'So, good luck to you, Sara Ravenscroft,' he said to himself as they walked towards the house in amicable silence. 'One thing's certain, *you* aren't the sort of girl to let a man down when he's in trouble, so here's hoping Redvers has seen the last of Miranda. It would never do for her to come barging into his life again just when the right girl has come along.' And he glanced appreciatively at his slender companion who little guessed what was going on in his head. Had he given her a clue she would have felt considerably cheered. The immediate future might look bleak but, with both Guy and Caroline gunning for her, in the long run she simply couldn't lose.

Or could she?

Fate is notoriously unpredictable and, with the situation as it was, the outcome would all depend on Miranda.

★   ★   ★

When Sara came downstairs the next morning the two men were nowhere to be seen but the remains of their breakfast still littered the kitchen table. Mrs Foster had her own family to see to and she wasn't expected to put in an appearance before ten o'clock, so Sara piled the dirty crockery into the sink and, while she waited for the kettle to boil, she laid a tray for Caroline, lightly boiled an egg and cut some thin slices of bread and butter.

It was a glorious day and she was convinced that everything was going to work out all right. Guy would have explained to Redvers about the mix-up and she was hopeful that the atmosphere would soon become more relaxed.

But her optimism was short-lived. She had hardly poked her head round the office door when Redvers stormed in. 'I thought you said something about making an early start,' he remarked, glancing pointedly at the battery operated clock whose hands pointed to nine-thirty.

'The clock's fast,' she said defensively. 'It's only just nine o'clock and I had your mother's breakfast to see to, and all the muddle in the kitchen to clear away.'

'That's Mrs Foster's job, not yours,' he retorted. 'You'll find you have enough to do coping with the office work without running round the house with a mop and duster. That's one of the advantages of employing a male secretary — he doesn't get side-tracked by non-essentials.'

Sara bit her lip. Evidently Redvers was still smarting from the trick his mother had played on him and it was immaterial to him whether or not Sara had been a party to it. Either way he had no intention of letting her forget she was here on sufferance, and her only hope of getting on friendly terms with him was to prove she was every bit as efficient as her predecessor.

'If you'll show me what you want me to do I won't waste any more time,' she said, acting on the principle that a soft answer turneth away wrath.

'*I* don't know what you're supposed to do,' he answered with a gesture of exasperation. 'You'll have to sort it out for yourself.'

'Surely Mr Willis didn't leave the office in all this muddle?' she asked. 'He must have had some sort of method.'

'I daresay it looks worse than it is,' Redvers told her. 'Guy and I have been in once or twice to attend to urgent business so we may have disturbed some of the files, but it shouldn't take you long to put things right, so I'll leave you to it.'

Left to herself Sara stared round her

in dismay. She had never seen such chaos: papers littering the floor, drawers wedged half open, a badly typed half finished letter in the typewriter. What was she expected to do? Wave a magic wand?

Grim-faced she set to work, soon abandoning all attempt at solving Mr Willis's method. No doubt he himself knew where everything was kept but it offended Sara's sense of order to find invoices mixed up with unpaid bills and bank statements. As for his book-keeping, it was completely haphazard and, to judge by the number of crossing outs and alterations, it occurred to her that arithmetic was not his strong point. The only thing to do was to start from scratch and she concentrated on col-lecting together all the correspondence relating to the present year and sorting it into appropriate piles. This was very time-consuming and she had not made much headway when she was inter-rupted by Caroline who begged her to take a break for coffee.

'Don't be a silly girl — of course you can spare five minutes,' she admonished, leading the way into the garden where a table and four chairs had been arranged in front of the summer house. 'I've told Mrs Foster to go and fetch the menfolk, but she doesn't seem to think they'll come. So foolish of them not to have a sit-down half way through the morning. They'll ruin their digestions as well as driving themselves into an early grave. How are you getting on with the work, Sara? Have you broken the back of it?'

'Not so as you'd notice,' Sara admitted, sitting on the edge of her chair and gulping down her coffee. 'There's heaps to do and I haven't got the hang of it yet.'

'There's always to-morrow,' Caroline reminded her. 'Sit back and relax, my dear. You'll work better for a short rest.'

At that moment Mrs Foster returned from her wasted journey across the field. 'Told you,' she said laconically. 'They say it's all right for *some*, but others has work to do.'

Sara jumped guiltily to her feet. Anyone in the nearest greenhouse had an uninterrupted view of the garden and she was sure Redvers had seen her taking time off to drink coffee when she should have been closeted in the office.

The rest of the morning flew by on wings but by one o'clock she had made definite headway, and she was glancing round the office with a feeling of satisfaction when the dinner gong sounded.

'Well done,' said Guy's voice from the doorway. 'You've worked wonders.'

She smiled her thanks, wishing it could have been his partner who had spoken but knowing that it would be many a long day before Redvers would condescend to sing her praises.

'I'm beginning to see daylight,' she nodded as they joined the others in the dining-room. 'Last month's invoices are still missing but I expect they'll turn up.'

'Who cares if they don't?' Caroline

chimed in. 'Your responsibilities begin as from to-day and you must look on the time that Mr Willis has been ill as the Bermuda Triangle.'

'Very convenient,' Redvers remarked dryly, 'but if we can't trace a certain prestigious order from Lord Somebody-or-other for five hundred yellow roses for his daughter's wedding next Saturday, we shall be badly out of pocket. I've looked high and low for it but it's completely vanished.'

'Surely you can remember the name and address?' Caroline asked.

'Don't be dumb, Mother. If I could remember it there'd be no problem. I know Willis wrote confirming the order so it's going to cause a great deal of inconvenience if the roses don't turn up. And don't tell me to look in *Burke's Peerage* because that wouldn't help. I'm hopeless when it comes to remembering names and so is Guy. It's a nasty headache because, once you've let down a customer, you get a bad name.' There was an edge to his voice which did not escape Sara's notice and she vowed to redouble her efforts to find not only the missing invoices but also the important order from 'Lord Somebody-or-other'.

She eventually found the invoices in a folder which had become wedged behind a half open drawer but there was still no trace of the order and she was on the verge of despair when a sudden thought struck her. There could well be some mention of a forthcoming society wedding in the London newspapers and, remembering Redvers had been engrossed in a crossword puzzle on the train, she was pretty certain he would have a daily delivery of *The Times*. Mrs Foster had not yet returned to cook the evening meal but Sara guessed the back numbers of newspapers would be stowed away in the cupboard under the stairs. This proved to be the case and she returned to the office with a dozen copies which she leafed through with all speed. She soon found what she was looking for and a telephone call to the London residence of the bride-to-be's father confirmed she had the right address and that the delivery of five hundred Diorama roses was expected on the eve of the wedding.

Satisfied that she had done a good day's work she fetched a duster, the vacuum cleaner and a dustpan and brush and, having emptied the waste paper basket, she swept several old cobwebs off the ceiling before attempting to remove the accumulated dust of many years. Evidently Mrs Foster had been forbidden to set foot in the office, which was a pity because it was a light, airy room and, if the furniture was polished and vases of flowers arranged on the window sill, it could be a pleasant place to work in. Had the windows ever been opened, she wondered, dubiously surveying the ancient sashcords. Better not risk it until they'd been checked. Perhaps she could ask Nathan Bond, who appeared to be the odd job man, and who she felt she already knew from Redvers's descriptions in his letters. 'Quite a character, is Nathan', he had written and, at the time, she had wondered if she would ever have the pleasure of meeting the knowledgeable old countryman.

Now for the vacuum cleaner. She switched it on and, pushing the furniture to one side, she set to work with a will. This proved to be a rewarding task because, as the dust was sucked up into the bag, the pattern on the carpet was revealed in all its glory and she found herself looking at what was undoubtedly a very valuable Persian carpet.

The noise of the vacuum cleaner prevented her from hearing Redvers come into the room and, when he spoke, she nearly jumped out of her skin. 'What do you think you're doing?' he asked, angrily pulling the plug out of the socket. 'I thought you agreed not to waste time on non-essentials.'

She felt her own anger rising. 'It's after office hours,' she pointed out in icy tones. 'Surely I'm allowed to amuse myself as I like in my spare time? This room is absolutely filthy and I don't appreciate breathing in dust eight hours a day.'

'Mr Willis never complained,' Redvers replied.

'Mr Willis happens to be a man, as you never tire of telling me,' she retorted. 'I expect he smoked like a chimney, and his lungs were so furred up he never noticed the stuffy atmosphere. And, while we're on the subject, I'd like to be able to open those windows.'

Redvers's look was one of sheer exasperation. 'Don't tell me you're a fresh-air fiend,' he gumbled. 'Women don't seem to realize the proper place for fresh air is out of doors. Mrs Foster spends half her time opening windows.'

'I wonder she dares,' Sara remarked. 'Working for ogres like you and Guy must be a pretty daunting experience.'

For a moment Redvers looked taken aback and then, for the first time since

Sara's arrival, his features relaxed into a smile. It was like sunshine after storm and Sara's heart leaped for joy. Was this the longed-for break-through, she wondered, or was it merely a temporary lull?

'Our bark is worse than our bite,' he told her, going over to the window and pulling back the catch. After a moment he succeeded in pushing up the lower pane and the resulting blast of fresh air blew a pile of papers onto the floor. 'There you are, there's nothing wrong with it,' he continued, 'but I'll get Nathan to ease the cords with some candle wax. It's bound to be stiff after all this time. I suppose you didn't find that order by any chance?' She shook her head and his shoulders drooped dispondently. 'Oh, well, it can't be helped. It's just that I hate letting a customer down.'

She knelt to retrieve the papers from the floor and, in silence, handed him the cutting from the society column. He glanced at it briefly and then his face lit up. 'Of course,' he exclaimed, clapping a hand to his forehead. 'Whyever didn't I think of it myself?'

'It takes brains,' she said, giving him a mischievous glance. 'I phoned to make certain there was no mistake and the secretary sounded a little puzzled because she had already received a letter of confirmation. So I told her Mr Willis has been taken ill and that I'm filling in on a temporary basis. I hope I did the right thing?'

'At least you know how to use your initiative,' he said, rather grudgingly, 'but kindly don't use the phone more than necessary. Calls to England are expensive and must be made only in an emergency. Is that understood? Idle chit-chat to friends could cost pounds.'

Sara reddened, wishing she hadn't had the temerity to be flippant. Evidently Redvers was quite determined to keep her in her place. 'I would naturally expect to pay for any personal calls,' she said. 'Not that the need will often arise. Your mother is more likely to run up a big bill than I am.'

Redvers frowned. 'I'll have a word with her about it,' he said. 'She can hardly expect Guy to foot the bill for her extravagance. The whole business of her being here is extremely worrying. If I'd known earlier in the season that she was coming I could have booked her in at a hotel or guest house, but they're all bursting at the seams.' He ran his hands through his hair in a characteristic gesture of irritation. 'If she decides to stay I can see many difficulties looming ahead. She'll be bored out of her mind and I fear she'll make many demands on your time. One thing she's got to realize — you have come here to work as a secretary and not as her companion, and she mustn't expect you to be at her beck and call. Office work must be your first consideration, otherwise the whole set-up will be a shambles. Willis was invariably tied to his desk from nine till five and, even then, he often had to put in overtime. Not that he grumbled. He was completely dedicated to his work and it will be well-nigh impossible to replace him.'

Sara looked round at the tidy office where everything was slotted neatly into place. The drawers could now open and shut, files were sorted out and the shelves were in apple-pie order — a very different set-up from the one which had greeted her on arrival. 'If you'll excuse me saying so,' she said with meticulous politeness, 'you really only need a part-time secretary. If Mr Willis had put his mind to it he could have finished all the paperwork by eleven o'clock and he could have spent the rest of the day helping you and Guy outdoors. As far as I can judge he must have spent most of his time with his feet up, smoking his pipe or resting his eyes. Far be it from me to criticize,' she continued, 'but it seems to me that your blue-eyed boy was a born muddler. I guarantee I could get through the work in a couple of hours, which would leave me with plenty of time for coffee breaks and entertaining your mother. 'Even,' she added wistfully, 'for helping in the greenhouses.'

'Indeed?' he said sceptically. 'Well, I'm delighted to hear it. We could certainly do with another pair of hands, though I imagine you know little or nothing about market gardening.'

'I'm supposed to have green fingers,' she told him.

'Green fingers? There's no such thing.' He spoke derisively. 'Gardening is a science. If you follow the rules you'll get results, and it's a complete myth to say that plants will grow for some people but not for others.'

She hid a smile. 'I gather you don't believe in talking to the flowers?' she asked.

'I certainly do not,' he replied.

'I've tried it,' she insisted, 'and it works. It really does. It might surprise you to discover what a little love and tenderness will do.'

His glance swept over her, noting the brightness of her eyes, and the way her mouth turned upward at the corners. It was a mouth that might be very pleasant to kiss, alluring, innocently seductive, and he had a sudden overpowering urge to take her in his arms and press his lips against hers. He had sworn never again to be taken in by a woman's wiles but Sara had made no attempt to flirt with him, and there was a world of sincerity in her voice when she spoke of love and tenderness. But could he trust this gentle girl, he wondered, or would she turn out to be a second Miranda, alike not only in looks but also in character?

His mouth twisted sardonically as he remembered how he had rushed head-long into an affair with Miranda. He certainly wasn't going to make the same mistake again, but surely it wouldn't matter if he lowered his guard a little?

'It's an interesting theory,' he remarked. 'Prove it if you can but I warn you I'll take a lot of convincing.' And, turning on his heel, he hurried out of the room,

leaving Sara to wonder if he was refer-
ring to the language of flowers or human
beings.

'Prove it if you can,' he had said.

'Well, I will,' she vowed, lifting her
chin defiantly. 'There's nothing —
absolutely nothing — that a little love
and tenderness can't achieve.'

7

To Redvers's surprise his mother showed no sign of being bored. Indeed, she laughingly declared she hadn't been so busy since she left Abbotsfield. 'I was in danger of becoming a social parasite,' she confessed, 'but now I'm a woman again, housewife, gardener, chief packager, amateur golfer — and mother.' She gave Redvers a fond glance. 'You can't think how rewarding it is to be living under the same roof with you again,' she continued. 'To darn your socks and sew on your buttons, to see that you eat proper meals and go to bed at a reasonable hour.'

'I wonder you don't insist on washing my neck and behind my ears,' he teased. During the past week his manner had become more relaxed and he was beginning to recover his sense of humour, which had been noticeably absent since the plane crash. Guy welcomed the change in him, pleased that his somewhat moody partner was becoming quite human. Being an observant man he realized this was largely Sara's doing and not Caroline's, and he confidently hoped that Redvers would fall in love with the pretty self-effacing girl who clearly adored him.

All four of them spent a considerable amount of time in the greenhouses and packing-shed, while old Nathan pottered about in the fields, waging constant war on green fly, black fly, caterpillars and slugs. Caroline found she had a flair for packing flowers and she had taken the responsibility of boxing the five hundred yellow roses which had been ordered for the prestigious society wedding.

The buds were picked in the early afternoon and Guy was taking them to the airport to ensure they would arrive at their destination in perfect condition. Unfortunately, at the very last minute, he cut his hand on a piece of glass and, as the wound needed stitching, Sara offered to drive him to the hospital and leave him there while she went on to the airport with the flowers.

'Please let me go,' she said, saving Redvers the embarrassment of having to ask her to do him a favour. Neither Caroline nor Nathan could drive and no way was he going to the airport himself, so, without Sara's help, the roses would have been completely wasted, resulting in a serious financial loss.

Guy's hand was slow to heal and, as there were several rush orders to be attended to during the next few days, it was taken for granted that Sara would drive the estate car to the airport. She enjoyed these breaks from the daily routine and she would sometimes deliberately return a long way round in order to familiarize herself with every aspect of the island which she had grown to love. She drove slowly past cottages and farms, delighting in the abundance of scent and colour, but it was the sight of the turbulent sea frothing over the jagged rocks that really fascinated her and, despite Redvers's warning as to the hidden dangers, she often scrambled down to the shore where she would wander, heedless of time, gathering a vast assortment of shells. The decorative cowrie took pride of place in her collection and Guy would often tease her, telling her she should take a wheelbarrow with her instead of a small holdall.

One morning Caroline surprised everyone, including herself, by announcing she would like to take a trip to one of the off-shore islands. 'But, Mother,' Redvers protested, 'you know what a rotten sailor you are. You can't even go on a rowing-boat without feeling sick.'

'If I'm going to live on a small island like St Mary's it's a phobia I shall have to try and overcome,' Caroline said firmly. 'After all, that's what seasickness is — a phobia. I've been afraid of boats ever since I was a child and went out fishing with your grandfather and nearly drowned.'

'Seasickness is not a phobia,' Redvers said. 'It's to do with the balance of the ear.'

'In my case it's a phobia,' Caroline insisted, 'and, as such, I'm going to fight it. We could try Samson to start with. It's only a short distance away and I've been looking at those launches which operate from St Mary's Quay. They look as safe as houses and, if we choose a calm day, I'm quite sure I shall be all right. Later on we can go further afield, to Bryher, Tresco and St Martin's, and to the little uninhabited islands to see the seals and sharks.'

'Your enthusiasm does you credit,' Redvers said dryly. 'Who do you hope will accompany you on these trips? We're all far too busy to spare the time, though I've noticed Sara isn't a dedicated clock watcher. She's been known to take half a day driving home from the airport whereas Guy can do the same journey in twenty minutes.'

'Sara's a sensible girl,' Caroline observed. 'Life shouldn't be one mad rush. The poet knew what he was talking about when he wrote: 'What is this life if, full of care, we have no time to stand and stare'. In any case, Sara doesn't neglect her duties. She deals with all the correspondence in half the time it took Mr Willis, and you must admit she's invaluable in the greenhouses and packing-shed. She deserves a break.'

Redvers frowned. 'So you intend to take Sara with you on these expeditions?'

'I intend all four of us to go,' Caroline stated. 'There's absolutely no reason why you can't down tools occasionally and leave Nathan to cope on his own. He's perfectly capable, and I'd like to know when you last took a day off. Not since you visited me in Brighton in May, I'll be bound. You know the saying 'all work and no play makes Jack a dull boy'. Well, that's what's happening to you. You can't talk about anything except flowers, fruit and vegetables.'

'There could be worse subjects,' Redvers remarked dryly.

'Yes, but you shouldn't discuss gardening to the exclusion of all else,' Caroline argued. 'If you don't scintillate occasionally Sara will go looking for a new boss and then where will you be? Well and truly in the soup because you'll never find anyone to take her place.'

The truth of this remark struck home. Redvers was beginning to appreciate how invaluable Sara was and the thought of losing her was insupportable. Not only was she a willing and efficient worker, she was also a joy to have around the place. So many things about her endeared her to him — her fondness for Caroline and her never-ending patience even when the older woman was at her most trying; her funny little habit of talking to the flowers; the sound of her voice, and the lilt of her laughter. Yes, he would miss her very much if she left. Nonetheless, he had no intention of giving way to his feelings. It was early days yet and for the time being his relationship with Sara must remain strictly on a business footing. Admittedly it was two years since his split with Miranda but some wounds are slow to heal and his trust in the female sex had received such a severe battering it would be many a long day before he recovered from the trauma of being jilted.

However, there could be no harm in going for a boat trip, provided it was a foursome and not a twosome, and he found himself looking forward to a break from the normal routine. Saturday morning dawned sunny and warm and, while he waited for the womenfolk to finish preparing food for the picnic, he walked across the greenhouse field to have a final word with Nathan.

It was while he was away that the post arrived and Caroline went into the front hall to collect it. She was standing motionless, with the letters in her hand, when Sara came out of the kitchen, and there was such a strange expression on her face that Sara was instantly concerned.

'Aren't you feeling very well?' she asked, taking Caroline's arm and leading her towards the oak settle. 'Sit down and I'll fetch you a drink of water.'

'No, I'm perfectly all right,' Caroline replied in a strangled voice. 'But look at this letter — it's from Miranda.'

The handwriting on the pale blue envelope was all too familiar and Sara's heart dropped like a stone. Somehow or other Miranda must have got hold of Redvers's address and no doubt she had written in the hope of arranging a reunion.

'Thank God it was I who found the letter and not Redvers,' Caroline continued, as, with shaking fingers, she stowed it away in her handbag. 'I shall destroy it as soon as possible.'

Sara stared at her in amazement.

'You can't do that,' she protested. 'Redvers would never forgive you for interfering in his affairs.'

'He need never know,' Caroline replied. 'If this letter is ignored, even Miranda won't have the effrontery to write again.'

Knowing Miranda, Sara thought it very unlikely she would give up so easily but, in any case, she had no wish to be a party to the deception. 'Please give it to me,' she said, holding out her hand for the letter. 'I'll put it in the office with the other post and he can read it when we get back. You never know, he may choose to ignore it.'

'That's a forlorn hope, my dear,' Caroline contradicted. 'I'm convinced he still cares for her and, given the chance, he'll be perfectly happy to forgive and forget.'

'Then you've no right to interfere,' Sara argued. 'Please give it to me,' she repeated desperately. 'If he finds out Miranda has written, he'll think I kept the letter from him deliberately and he'll be so angry he'll give me the sack.'

But Caroline was adamant. Despite Sara's pleas she kept her handbag firmly shut and, when the girl persisted, her face became ashen and she had such difficulty with her breathing that a heart attack seemed imminent. Eventually Sara agreed with the utmost unwillingness to say nothing about the letter but it was with a feeling of impending doom that she went out to the car. It took her some time to shake off her depression, though she couldn't help feeling glad that Redvers hadn't read the letter before they set out, or the day would have been completely spoilt. His thoughts would have been so taken up with Miranda he would have had little time to spare for his immediate companions and they would have been robbed of what proved to be a most enjoyable trip.

Half way over to Samson, Caroline declared she was feeling fine and would just as soon go on to Raffin Island and see the gulls, and then to Bryher,

Tresco and St Martin's.

'Aren't you being a bit wholesale?' Redvers laughed. 'I suggest we go to the sub-tropical gardens in Tresco and give everywhere else a miss. You really need a whole day to enjoy each separate island and there's no sense in rushing things.'

It sounded as if he intended to make this trip the first of many and presently Sara relaxed, determined to live one day at a time.

And certainly this was a day to remember. Afterwards her most vivid recollection was of a brief interlude she spent alone with Redvers in an unsequestered corner of the gardens. The other two were ahead of them, and she had hung back to admire a beautiful stone archway almost hidden by flowers, while Redvers waited, a shade impatiently, for her to follow.

'It's so lovely here,' she breathed. 'And to think I almost didn't come.'

He surprised her by coming to stand by her side, his hand resting lightly on the sun-warmed stone above her head. 'I'm glad you did,' he said.

She waited, with held breath, wondering what was coming next, and she felt oddly deflated when he continued in a matter-of-fact voice. 'My mother would never have visited me if you hadn't come too, and she looks so much better than the last time I saw her. The calm atmosphere of the Scillies makes it a wonderful place for getting rid of stresses and strains.'

Sara had never stood so close to him before and his nearness caused her heart beats to quicken and the palms of her hands grow moist. Her love had grown hungry for recognition and desperately she willed him to respond with an ardour equal to her own. The intenseness of her longing must have communicated itself to him because, a moment later, she was in his arms, their heart beats matching as his mouth probed hers in a kiss so sweet, so passionate, she was transported to those realms of unbelievable bliss where previously she had only travelled in imagination.

Guy's voice calling for them to hurry brought them back to *terra firma* and Redvers released her abruptly, leaving her to wonder whether he was already regretting what was probably only an impulsive action on his part.

Soon after they got home, Caroline came into Sara's bedroom and, without preamble, said she had opened Miranda's letter. 'She got my forwarding address from that stupid woman, Charmaine Lessimore,' she said and her face was flushed with righteous anger. 'It didn't take her long to put two and two together and guess I was staying with Redvers. The letter is couched in very affectionate terms, mixed up with a lot of sob stuff. To cut a long story short, she wants to heal the breach and she begs to be allowed to come and see him. You can guess the sort of blah. Her marriage was a disaster. Her husband was cruel to her. She has never loved anyone but Redvers and bitterly regrets breaking off their engagement. The letter is full of apologies and excuses and calculated to soften a far harder heart than Redvers's.' Caroline's eyes flashed and her lips became a thin line. 'I've torn it up,' she continued, 'and put the pieces in the refuse bin.'

Despite her fear of incurring Caroline's displeasure Sara thought it imperative to sound a note of warning. 'When she doesn't hear from him she won't let it rest at that,' she declared. 'She'll be sure to write again.'

'But not immediately,' Caroline insisted. 'We have several days, perhaps even a week, to think up a plan to thwart her.'

Sara flinched. She objected to the use of that royal 'we', but it was a waste of time to point out that she herself had been against concealing the letter. 'I can't think of anything,' she confessed. 'Miranda strikes me as being a very determined young woman.'

'Yes, but supposing he marries someone else — that would spike her guns,' Caroline gloated. 'It's what I've had in mind ever since I first set eyes on you and I'm sure you would have no objections to carrying out my wishes. Anyone with half an eye can see you're madly in love with him. And think of the advantages, my dear. Marriage to Redvers would make your future secure because, on your own admittance, you have no home of your own.'

'That's not true,' Sara contradicted. 'My father would love to have me live with him again.'

'But not your stepmother,' Caroline persisted. 'You left home once because of her — would you really like to go back? And I suspect you have no real friends in your home town. I have never tried to pry into your affairs but I have always felt there must be something behind your precipitous flight from Bristol, else why no letters or telephone calls?'

She paused to let her words sink in and Sara's face became drained of colour. Under no circumstances would she reveal her past to Caroline.

'I don't know why you're making a mystery of my coming to Brighton,' she said with a show of bravado. 'I wanted a change of scene and Miss Benson offered me a better job — that's all there is to it.'

'Just as you say, dear,' Caroline replied, maddening Sara with her look of patent disbelief. 'But that's beside the point. Every girl wants to get married and you're admirably suited to life in the Scillies.'

'Are you thinking of my happiness or are you merely making this suggestion out of spite?' Sara asked with ill-concealed bitterness. 'You want to get your own back on Miranda, don't you?'

'Yes, but only incidentally,' Caroline replied. 'My chief concern is for Red-vers. He has suffered enough from that selfish, unprincipled girl and I'm sure you would make an ideal wife for him.'

'But he still loves Miranda — you said so yourself,' Sara pointed out. 'I don't fancy marrying a man whose affections are otherwise engaged.'

'Then it's up to you to disengage those affections,' Caroline said with one of her sweetest smiles.

'It's the woman who leads the man to the altar and not the other way round, though, I warn you, you'll have to be circumspect. Redvers is very astute and if he suspects for a single moment that you're after him, you won't see him for dust.'

'I won't do it,' Sara said stubbornly. 'I've too much self-respect to go running after a man, so you'll have to think of some other way of getting Redvers out of Miranda's clutches. And now, if you'll excuse me, I'm going to have a bath.'

'Very well,' said Caroline, immediately taking umbrage. 'If you won't co-operate, you won't, but I'm extremely disappointed in you.' And so saying, she flounced out of the room, completely forgetting to play her usual trump card. Not that it would have done her much good because Sara was beginning to suspect that Caroline's blood pressure was nowhere near danger level and that the older woman often made use of her supposed illness as a form of blackmail.

To let it be known she was still annoyed with Sara, Caroline refused to come down to the evening meal. She sent a message via Mrs Foster, saying she was tired after their long day and would have her supper in bed and then an early night.

'I hope it's nothing to worry about,' Redvers remarked. 'She's seemed so much better lately but I daresay she walked too far, and the boat trip must have been an ordeal, although she made light of it.'

'At least she wasn't ill,' Sara reminded him, 'so her seasickness probably *is* a phobia.'

'She's a brave woman to fight it,' Guy observed, with a meaning look in Redvers's direction. 'I always say one should face up to one's fears and then they disappear.'

Redvers raised an eyebrow. 'Stop getting at me, Guy,' he said with a hint of irritability in his voice and, turning to Sara, he pointedly changed the subject.

'You see how it is with him', Guy said afterwards to Sara. 'He absolutely refuses to discuss his phobia about flying.'

'Does it matter?' she countered. 'The necessity for him to go in an aeroplane is never likely to arise, so what's the point of getting himself worked up?'

'That's an ostrich attitude,' Guy argued. 'Until Redvers gets over his phobia he'll go on having these dreadful nightmares — or 'day' mares, if there is such a word. Fortunately we live away from the flight path but I wouldn't like you to see him on one of the few occasions when a low-flying plane passes directly overhead.'

It did not take much imagination on Sara's part to conjure up a picture of a man driven almost demented by the sound he had grown to dread, bringing, as it did, a stark reminder of the crash in which he had so nearly lost his life. 'What would be your solution to the problem?' she asked.

'He could attend one of those group sessions which specialize in getting rid of the deep-seated fear of flying,' Guy answered, 'or, better still, he could book a flight to the mainland and force himself to get on a plane or helicopter. Once he was airborne he'd find it a piece of cake. If he could have flown immediately after the crash he'd have been okay, like getting on a horse as soon as you've been thrown, but he was in hospital for weeks and then it was too late. His phobia had taken root and now it's going to be the very devil to cure him.'

Sara nodded. 'But we can't interfere,' she said. 'Redvers is the last person to take advice, even from well-meaning friends, so it's up to him to work out his own salvation. I'm sure he has sufficient strength of character to win through in the end.'

Guy gave her a knowing glance. 'You really admire him, don't you?' he asked.

She met his look without flinching.

'Yes, I do,' she replied. 'I think he's the most wonderful man in the world.'

The next morning Caroline was herself again, all sweetness and light, and she made no reference to the topic she and Sara had quarrelled about. Whether she had another plan for 'spiking Miranda's guns', Sara did not know, and she certainly wasn't going to raise the subject of her own free will.

Meanwhile her relationship with Redvers was subtly changing. The memory of their kiss still lingered and, although Sara did not consciously set out to attract, human nature stepped in and she found she was taking that little bit of extra time on her appearance. Redvers, too, began to respond more warmly to her femininity, to bark at her less often, and to take the trouble to thank her occasionally for the many extra services she perfomed apart from her secretarial duties.

Caroline sat in the wings and purred, certain her advice had borne fruit and that, despite her denials, Sara was doing exactly as she had asked her to do. 'Hurry, hurry,' she wanted to say. 'Speed is the essence', and she went to endless ploys to ensure that the young couple spent as much time alone together as possible.

'My mother's a born matchmaker,' Redvers said on one occasion. 'I suppose she thinks I'm blind to what she's up to. Still, I must say I find your company extremely pleasant after two years undiluted diet of Guy and Nathan.'

'I'm glad I'm giving satisfaction, *sir*,' she answered, matching his light mood with her own.

He chuckled. 'That reminds me of the first evening you were here,' he remembered, 'when you called me 'sir'. It really got under my skin.'

'It was meant to,' she confessed. 'I wanted to pay you out for being so beastly to me.'

'Was I?' he laughed. 'Well, you must admit it was a bit of a facer having a girl secretary thrust on me when I specifically asked for a man.'

'That was Caroline's fault, not mine,' she reminded him. 'I honestly didn't know about it. You do believe me, don't you, Redvers?'

'I do now, but I didn't at the time,' he answered, suddenly becoming serious. 'You'd never lie to me, would you, Sara? That's one of the things I like about you. You're always honest.'

It was the end of the day and they were strolling back across the fields after watching the sunset, a walk that was fast becoming a nightly ritual. Suddenly Sara stumbled and she would have fallen if Redvers hadn't caught her. A moment later he was holding her in a fierce embrace, his kisses kindling a flame inside her which spread like wildfire through her veins, and it is a matter of debate how long they would have remained there, with their bodies fused against each other, if a rabbit had not darted across the soft, spongy turf, almost butting into them in its hurry.

'We seem fated to be disturbed,' Redvers murmured with a rueful chuckle. 'First by Guy in the Tresco Gardens and now by a damned rabbit. Perhaps next time we shall be luckier.' He released her reluctantly, though not before he had trailed his mouth along the slender column of her throat, arousing in her once more the intoxicating flames of desire.

Afterwards Sara wasn't sure whether the interruption was a good thing or a bad. If Redvers had really been such an ardent lover as he appeared to be, he wouldn't have let a little thing like a rabbit interfere with his enjoyment, so perhaps he had welcomed the diversion and been grateful to the little animal for bringing him to his senses before he made a complete fool of himself.

'If there *is* a next time I'll make certain it's not at my invitation,' Sara vowed. 'Redvers will never get around to asking me to marry him if he thinks I'm doing the chasing, so the next step must definitely come from him. But how much time have I got before Miranda appears on the scene?'

The thought of Redvers's ex-fiancée was a continual source of worry to her and she waited on tenterhooks for the girl's next move, because she was quite convinced that Miranda would sooner or later cause trouble. Sure enough, the next morning another letter arrived and this time it was Redvers who collected the post. Without looking at it he brought it into the office and dumped it on the desk for Sara to sort through.

'Anything of interest?' he asked, watching her as she picked out the business letters and put them on one side.

'Mostly bills,' she answered, avoiding his eyes. The memory of last night's kiss was still so vivid that his nearness unnerved her and she was afraid to smile in case he thought she was encouraging him to carry on where he left off. 'These are the personal ones,' she continued. 'Two for your mother and one for you.'

The one for Redvers was from Miranda and, try as she would, Sara could not keep the tremor out of her voice at sight of the all too familiar handwriting. She was sure Redvers would notice her distress but he took the letter from her without comment and, going over to the window, he slit open the envelope. As he read the contents a frown furrowed his brow and, turning to Sara, he asked her if she had any recollection of a similar letter. Torn between her desire to tell the truth and her fear of unpleasant repercussions, she remained tongue-tied and, when he impatiently repeated his question, she dumbly shook her head, pretending to be engrossed in the rest of the mail.

'It's very odd,' he remarked. 'Surely it couldn't have got lost in the post?'

Feeling she should say something she asked if it was important and was filled with an overwhelming sense of relief when he replied that it didn't matter in the least, though something in the savage way in which he tore the second letter into shreds, told her that both letters had mattered very much. Taking a steadying breath she managed to control her trembling limbs, but she was still in a state of near collapse when he crossed the room in two strides and, putting his hands on her shoulders, he stared deeply into her eyes.

'Since we are extremely unlikely to be interrupted by a rabbit this morning,' he began, 'how about continuing where we left off last night?'

She tried to back away from him but he held her in a grip of iron.

'Guy — or your mother — might come in,' she stammered, glancing over her shoulder.

'No need to worry. I have taken the precaution of locking the door.' His breath was warm on her face and as he moved his hands from her shoulders to slide them round her waist, she felt her senses reel.

'I want you,' he groaned. 'I need you. Will you marry me, Sara? Will you be my wife?'

Her heart leaped with joy but,

although her lips moved, she could not answer. Despite her feeling of elation she was filled also with a sense of dread. Why was he asking her to marry him? She was sure marriage was the last thing he had in mind when he kissed her the previous evening, so why was he now so desperately anxious to put a ring on her finger? It didn't make sense.

Commonsense told her she should refuse his request but she loved him deeply, passionately and utterly — loved him in the way that Elizabeth Barrett Browning had so beautifully described: 'I love thee with the breath, smiles, tears of all my life', and there was no way she could fight against it. Yes, she would agree to marry him whatever his reason for asking.

She hardly realized she had nodded in assent but the look on his face told her she had committed herself. 'Soon?' he said urgently. 'Promise me it will be soon. This week if we can arrange it. I'll get a special licence.'

'Yes,' she agreed, her senses still swimming, 'I'll marry you as soon as you like.'

But even as she spoke she was again shaken by a sense of dread. There was something behind this fever of impatience that boded ill for their future happiness. But it was a dread she couldn't put a name to and, she determinedly blotted it out of her mind.

'There's nothing to fear,' she told herself. 'I always knew my destiny was linked with Redvers and marriage will ensure the link will never be broken, so what's the matter with me? I should be on cloud nine instead of in this stupid dither.'

'I love you, Sara,' he said huskily and, as she surrendered herself once more to his kisses, she steadfastly stilled the small inner voice that mocked her, for would it not have been nearer the truth if he had said: 'I love you, Miranda'? And was he not merely using her as a shield against a love that had once betrayed him?

8

The honeymoon was as perfect as a honeymoon could be and Sara's only complaint was that it was far too short, but Redvers said that five days and four nights was all the holiday he was justified in taking, even though Guy assured him the business would not collapse if he stayed away for twice that length of time.

Five days of warm companionship. Four nights of bliss. From Sara's point of view it was over far too quickly and, as she and Redvers boarded *Scillonian* for the final stage of their homeward journey, she could not help but wonder what lay ahead of them, for she was convinced the even tenor of their lives would shortly be disrupted by Miranda from whom, as far as she knew, nothing had been heard since the arrival of her second letter which Redvers had savagely destroyed.

Their honeymoon had been spent touring the West Country and it was Redvers's suggestion that they should call and see her father. If he had thought it strange she did not invite any of her family or friends to the wedding, he had made no comment, and he had apparently accepted at its face value her excuse that the Scilly Isles were too far away for them to come, especially at such short notice.

Redvers and her father got along very well, and her stepmother behaved in a friendly fashion, making it difficult to believe that Sara had fled from home because of her animosity. Inevitably Bernard's name cropped up in conversation, her family taking it for granted she had told Redvers about her broken engagement and, when Irene let fall that he had recently returned from a spell at Stoke Mandeville Hospital, Sara felt Redvers's gaze resting thoughtfully upon her.

Afterwards he asked her why she had

made no mention of her broken engagement. 'As your future husband I think I had a right to know,' he said.

At this hint of male arrogance her anger rose. 'What about Miranda?' she demanded. 'You have never once mentioned her name to me.'

'That's quite different,' he replied. 'No doubt you heard all about her from my mother, whereas I have been left completely in the dark.'

'I didn't want to talk about it,' she excused herself. 'It was a time of great unhappiness for me. In any case, it's in the past.' But, even as she spoke, she was aware that the past has a habit of catching up with one and, blameless though she was, she would always carry a terrible burden of guilt.

Redvers did not refer to the subject again and the rest of their honeymoon flew by in perfect harmony. Their homecoming was a happy one, for Caroline welcomed them with undisguised joy and Guy, also, made it known how pleased he was to see them again. Naturally Sara would have preferred to come back to her own home but there had been no time to go house hunting before they were married, so they were temporarily obliged to go on living in Guy's house. They intended to start looking straightaway but it might be some while before a suitable property came on the market so, for the time being, Sara would have to resign herself to sharing a home with Guy and her mother-in-law.

She didn't mind about Guy: he was a bumbling old darling and in any case it was his home and it was very kind of him to make them welcome but, fond though she was of Caroline, she did not relish the idea of being under her continual scrutiny. Newly-weds need privacy, and tact was hardly her mother-in-law's strong point. However she seemed to have made up her mind to make life as pleasant as possible for them and, during their absence, she had moved her things out of the spacious guest room into the bedroom Redvers had been using. 'I shall be perfectly all right in here,' she declared when Sara voiced her concern. 'It's not as if it's a permanent arrangement because I, too, shall be looking for new accommodation — unless, of course, you and Redvers buy a really large house and provide me with a 'Granny flat'.'

Detecting a note of wistfulness in Caroline's voice, Sara felt a twinge of misgiving. On the face of it, it would be an ideal arrangement but it did not appeal to her in the slightest, though she could hardly say so in so many words.

'We shall have to have a family discussion,' she prevaricated. 'It will be up to Redvers to make the final decision.'

'Yes, of course,' Caroline agreed, 'though it's wonderful how a man can be tactfully coerced if a woman goes the right way about it. Take your marriage for instance. I've the greatest admiration for the way in which you inveigled Redvers to put a ring on your finger.'

Sara coloured. 'I wouldn't have thought 'inveigled' was the right word,' she said. 'I married Redvers for love and not for any other reason.'

'I know that, my dear, but you probably wouldn't have succeeded in rescuing him from Miranda's clutches if you hadn't taken my advice and practised your womanly arts on him. I shall never cease to be grateful to you for being so co-operative.'

Sara hid her exasperation as best she could, knowing it would be useless to argue. Whatever she said, Caroline would continue to think it was at her instigation that Sara had deliberately set out to catch Redvers and that, between them, they had engineered a plot which, happily, had come to a success-ful conclusion.

In honour of their homecoming Mrs Foster made a special effort to provide them with a slap-up evening meal, serving chilled cucumber soup made from her own secret recipe, followed by grilled mackerel, with marrowfat peas and butter-ball potatoes sprinkled with chopped parsley, and finishing with freshly picked raspberries and clotted cream. To celebrate the occasion Guy opened a bottle of home-made elderberry wine and it was so potent that Sara felt quite muzzy and Redvers suggested they should both go for a stroll to clear their heads.

But there were many chores to be seen to first and it was getting on for sundown before they set off across the greenhouse field in the direction of Carn Morval Point. This was one of Sara's favourite walks though, truth to tell, she could never be certain which she loved best. For such a small island there was an infinite variety of scene: during the daytime, when the weather was fine, the sea was crystal clear and it lapped gently onto beaches of fine white sand, or pounded against the rocks at Peninnis Head, enveloping the unwary onlooker in curtains of lacy spray. Inland the moors were gentle on the feet, for here the turf was soft and spongy, while along the rutted lanes, where honeysuckle and dog roses bloomed in profusion, the air was sweetly scented. But at eventide the view towards the western rocks was unforgettable and to-night, as always, Sara was struck dumb by its breathtaking magnificence.

Presently Redvers touched her shoulder. 'Listen,' he said, 'here comes Nathan on one of his nightly fishing expeditions.'

'Nathan?' she repeated. 'Surely he ought to be in bed and asleep?'

'He's like an old mule — he goes to sleep in the daytime standing up,' Redvers answered with a chuckle. 'Hadn't you noticed?'

Sara stifled a giggle; 'I always thought he was ruminating,' she said.

'That's the story he puts out,' Redvers replied, 'but who does he think he's fooling? Give him his due, he's worth his hire, and we'd miss all that nice fresh mackerel and pollock he supplies us with. Here he comes now, heading for the north-west channel.'

'You must have ears like a bat,' she said as the little fishing boat came into sight a few moments later. 'I never heard a thing.'

'Good hearing runs in the family,' he told her. 'I can hear a pin drop a mile away. Well, half a mile,' he conceded, seeing her look of disbelief. 'How's your head now? Still muzzy?'

'After all this sea air?' She laughed. 'No, I'm perfectly steady on my pins, thank you very much.'

His arm encircled her waist and he drew her close. 'It's better to be on the safe side,' he murmured, pressing his lips against the soft fragrance of her hair. She lifted her face to his and his mouth came down, lingering on her lips with a gentle persistence that quickened her pulses. To love and be loved — this was heaven indeed, and she sent up a little prayer that nothing, and nobody, would ever come between them.

For more than a week she was fooled into believing that her prayer was answered. The honeymoon atmosphere lingered on, and her cup of happiness was full when Redvers told her he had managed to find a furnished cottage for rent.

'When can we move?' she asked excitedly. 'Straightaway?'

'As soon as you like,' he said, 'Sorry I couldn't discuss it with you but I had to make up my mind on the spot, or someone else would have snapped it up.'

'I'm sure it'll be lovely,' she declared, overjoyed by the prospect of getting away from Caroline's ever watchful eye. 'Have you broken the news to your mother?' she added.

'Yes, and she was very understanding. She said she quite realized that love birds should have a nest to themselves.' He spoke a shade ironically. 'She seemed to think it was Guy who was the stumbling-block to our staying on here, so I didn't disillusion her.'

'I'm very fond of your mother . . . ' Sara protested.

'But not to the extent of living under the same roof with her,' he added. 'That goes for me, too.'

Sara sighed. 'You know she's hoping we'll buy a big house and provide her with a granny flat?' she asked.

'Don't worry. Something else may turn up,' he said philosophically.

Sara hoped it would but she wasn't very optimistic. Caroline usually got her own way and she had learnt from experience that one might as well give in to her first as last. Meanwhile she would enjoy having Redvers to herself, and she fell in love with the cottage at first sight.

'It's a darling little place,' she exclaimed, looking out of the casement window of what was to be their bedroom. 'What a picture to wake up to every morning.'

'The loneliness doesn't bother you?' he asked. 'It's a very different life here from the one you've been accustomed to.'

'I love it,' she said. 'To be living here

alone with you is my idea of paradise.'

His fingers gently traced the contour of her face, stopping momentarily at a point where a small frown creased her forehead. 'Is something troubling you?' he asked.

'Not really,' she sighed, 'but we do have a spare bedroom and your mother may want to come and stay with us straightaway instead of waiting till we get a larger house.'

'We're far too cramped,' he said. 'Think of all the luggage she brought with her. No, she'll be staying on at the big house for the time being. Luckily she and Guy seem to hit it off. In fact, their friendship has progressed considerably during our absence.'

'Redvers!' she exclaimed. 'You don't think . . . ?'

'I haven't got as far as that,' he smiled, 'but things have a way of working out for the best.'

They decided to move into the cottage that very same evening and this entailed making many journeys up and down stairs to collect their possessions. Caroline hovered near by, hindering rather than helping, and she waylaid Sara in the living-room when she was choosing some books from the well-stocked shelves. 'Still no word from Miranda,' she said in a conspiratoral whisper. 'I'm beginning to breathe freely at last, though I must say I'm amazed she gave up so easily. I tremble to think what might have happened if we hadn't intercepted her letter.'

Sara opened her mouth to point out that the deception had had nothing to do with her and that she had thoroughly disapproved of Caroline's action, but she remained silent, knowing her protest would fall on deaf ears.

'I rather thought the wretched girl might write again,' the older woman continued, 'but, when Redvers didn't reply, she evidently decided he had finished with her for good.'

'There *was* another letter,' Sara said rather reluctantly. 'It came the day Redvers asked me to marry him.'

'And you were able to intercept it? What a bit of luck!' Caroline's voice held a note of deep satisfaction. 'That makes it doubly certain we won't be hearing from Miss Miranda again.'

'I did nothing of the sort,' Sara flared. 'Redvers brought in the post and of course he read the letter.'

'Before you could stop him?' Caroline interrupted. 'Oh dear, that was a pity. I suppose Miranda mentioned she had already written and he must have wondered why he never got the letter. Did he ask you about it?'

'As a matter of fact, he did,' Sara replied, annoyed at this inquisition and biting her lip as she remembered the terrible moment when she had avoided answering Redvers's enquiry.

Caroline's face cleared. 'Obviously you didn't let on what we'd done or Redvers would have been furious,' she remarked approvingly. 'I presume you said the letter must have been lost in the post?'

This was too much for Sara. Seizing

a couple of books at random, she hurried from the room, only to bump full tilt into Redvers who was standing in the hall with his arms full of an assortment of clothes which he had been unable to cram into a suitcase.

'Redvers!' she stammered, knowing by the look on his face, that he had heard every word.

'For God's sake hurry up,' he said harshly and, pushing her on one side, he went out to the estate car where he sat rigidly in the driving seat until she joined him a few minutes later, followed by Guy and Caroline, who were completely unaware that anything was wrong.

'See you in the morning,' they called, waving a cheerful good-bye, and Sara forced herself to smile and wave back, though, in truth, her heart was as heavy as lead.

The drive to the cottage was completed in a silence which Sara was afraid to break in case she made matters worse but, when they had unpacked the car and dumped their possessions in the front hall, she turned to Redvers with an imploring gesture.

'Please listen to me,' she begged. 'What you overheard just now — it wasn't true. None of it. You must have jumped to the wrong conclusion.'

His eyes raked her from head to foot, making her feel about two inches tall. 'And what am I supposed to have overheard?' he asked, putting her to the torture of having to repeat what had been said.

'It wasn't I who intercepted Miranda's letter,' she faltered. 'It was your mother.'

'Indeed?' Ice could not have been colder than his voice. 'I gathered you were both in it together. You even went as far as lying to me by saying the letter must have got lost in the post.'

'I didn't lie to you,' she said in utter misery. 'I thought it best to remain silent for your mother's sake. I didn't want to make trouble between you.'

'How very noble,' he scoffed. 'And I

suppose you didn't deliberately set out to make me fall in love with you? No doubt my mother put you up to that, too. Well, you certainly played your part admirably.

'Stop it,' she cried, unable to bear it any longer. 'I love you, Redvers — doesn't that count for anything?'

'For what I am, or for what I can give you? Come off it, Sara. You planned your campaign from the first day we met at Abbotsfield. You admitted then that you had dreams of glory and, although you knew you could never be mistress of the manor, you decided you were on to a good thing. You cultivated my mother's friendship and managed to worm your way into her affections. Then, when you heard we wanted a secretary, you seized your opportunity to come chasing me here, persuading my mother to ignore the fact that we expressly asked for a man and not a girl to fill the post.'

'It's not true,' she wept. 'None of it's true. Redvers, you must believe me.

Our whole future happiness rests on mutual trust.'

Despite his anger, he could not help but pity her. She looked so small and vulnerable, and all his instincts cried out to him to take her in his arms and comfort her, but almost at once his resolve hardened. Even though it was evident that Caroline was largely to blame for the deception, Sara had been more than willing to go along with her, and he would not tolerate interference with his life. Therefore he remained withdrawn and Sara searched his face in vain for some softening in his attitude.

'Please believe me,' she whispered, but he merely shrugged his shoulders.

'One day perhaps,' he said non-committally. 'Time is a great healer.' And, without further discussion, he collected an armful of clothes and led the way upstairs.

He hesitated for only a moment outside the door of the double-bedded room and then proceeded along the landing to the spare room. He could not have made his meaning clearer if he had shouted it aloud. From now on they would be husband and wife in name only and there would be no repetition of the lovely intimacies they had shared on their honeymoon.

Wordlessly she turned away and went into the room where, only a few hours earlier, they had stood side by side, looking out of the window onto a scene of unsurpassed beauty. It was twilight now and the colours had faded into an over-all greyness that matched her mood. She wondered whether she would ever be happy again, but time, as Redvers had said, is a great healer and, even as the tears coursed down her cheeks, she was aware of a ray of hope. Somewhere, at the end of a long, dark tunnel, they would find happiness again. All that was needed was faith, hope — and a little tenderness.

Two days passed and she had almost reached breaking point when Redvers dropped a bombshell. Making no attempt to soften the blow he told her Miranda had phoned from the airport and he was meeting her in Hugh Town. They would have lunch together and then he would bring her back to the cottage.

Sara stared at him in stupefaction. 'Your ex-fiancée!' she exclaimed. 'Coming *here*? You must be joking!'

He shrugged. 'There's nowhere else for her to go,' he said. 'Can you imagine Mother putting up with her? You'd better get the spare room ready and I'll sleep downstairs.'

Without giving her a chance to reply he drove off in the direction of Hugh Town, leaving Sara seething, not only with Miranda but also with Redvers. How dare he behave like this? Would he go to any lengths to get his revenge for something that had, in fact, not been her fault at all?

Stony-faced she set about getting the room ready for the unwelcome guest, moving Redvers's things out of the wardrobe and chest of drawers and taking a perverse pleasure in making everything spotless, even picking some pinks and scabious and arranging them in a vase which she put on the bedside table.

When all was ready she ran downstairs and out of the cottage. She had no idea where she was going but of one thing she was certain — she would do anything, go anywhere, rather than act as hostess to her husband's ex-fiancée. She would even go back to England if need be. Her father's house was still home, and putting up with Irene's snide remarks would be preferable to the sort of treatment Redvers had been handing out to her ever since he overheard the unfortunate conversation between herself and Caroline.

Of course there was always Toby. Remembering her knight errant she was conscious of a lifting of the spirit, and the thought of his unswerving devotion brought a measure of comfort to her bruised heart. All she had to do was to pick up the telephone and tell him she needed him and he would come flying to her side, ready and willing to take care of her for the rest of her life.

But it was Redvers she loved, that arrogant, brooding man whose masculinity had the power to arouse in her the intoxicating flames of desire. Fond though she was of kind, uncomplicated Toby, he could never be a satisfactory substitute for the man she had married and from whom she was now estranged.

Busy with her thoughts she hadn't realized her footsteps had taken her in the direction of the market garden, and the sound of Guy's voice startled her. 'Who was that in the car with Redvers?' he asked. 'He drove by just now without stopping.'

'It was Miranda Sutcliffe,' she answered with forced casualness.

His eyes widened. 'Miranda Sutcliffe!' he repeated. 'Not the ghastly girl Redvers was once engaged to? What on earth is she doing in the Scillies?'

Sara shrugged. 'Your guess is as good

as mine,' she said. 'Perhaps she's come for a holiday.'

'That's a likely story,' Guy remarked caustically. 'You'll be saying next that Redvers invited her.'

'Well, he must have done, mustn't he?' Sara's voice was muffled as she fought for self-control. 'She would hardly have come otherwise.'

Gazing with concern at her ashen face, Guy took her by the arm and led her into the house. Seating her on the couch with a cushion behind her, he put his arm round her shoulders and waited for her to speak but, instead, she burst into tears, all the pent-up emotions of the last few days finding an outlet in a passion of weeping which alarmed him by its intensity.

'Suppose you tell me about it,' he said when at last the storm abated. 'Yes, everything,' he added sternly. 'There's no point in keeping anything from your uncle Guy.'

'I suppose not,' she said, with a watery smile. 'Everything's so awful I don't know how to bear it. And I don't know where to begin.'

'Why not start at the beginning?' he suggested.

'You know the beginning,' she said. 'It started the day I came here and Redvers was angry because he wanted a male secretary.'

'I think it started long before that,' Guy reminded her. 'Hadn't you already met Redvers and fallen in love with him? Wasn't that the real reason you came here? Not because Caroline persuaded you, but because you wanted to be part of Redvers's life.'

'Yes,' Sara admitted, 'but I had no intention of trapping him into marriage, which is what he accuses me of doing. He thinks I'm a scheming, double-crossing, two-timing bitch — though he hasn't said so in so many words.'

'I'm relieved to hear it,' Guy said, with a hint of dryness in his voice. 'It would be quite out of character for Redvers to swear at a lady. But let's get to the point. All was hunky-dory at your wedding and you were both starry-eyed when you came back from your honeymoon. What happened the day you moved into the cottage? I sensed there was something very wrong but it wasn't my business to pry into your affairs, so I could only stay on the sideline and hope that everything would work out all right. What happened, Sara? Why has Redvers asked Miranda to come and stay? On the face of it, it seems a sadistic thing to do and, again, that's out of character. Redvers has a hell of a temper but he hasn't got a spiteful bone in his body.'

'I don't blame him for being angry,' she whispered in a broken voice. 'He thinks I've deliberately interfered with his affairs, and you know how fiercely independent he is.' She paused, lifting brimming eyes to gaze in anguish at Guy's kindly face.

'Go on,' he said gently. 'Tell me the rest of the story.'

It was a relief to unburden herself.

She tried to be fair and not put all the guilt on Caroline's shoulders but Guy was shrewd enough to know that the blame lay entirely with Redvers's mother. Not that he stood in judgement. Caroline had only acted as she did to protect her son from the clutches of a wicked, scheming woman, substituting in her place a gentle, loving girl with whom Redvers would eventually find true happiness.

'I thoroughly approve of what Caroline did,' he declared. 'It's a great pity Redvers overheard your conversation and — yes, I don't wonder he was angry. But not to this extent. I can't believe Redvers would stoop to such a petty act of revenge. There's something at the bottom of it and it's up to me to find out what it is.'

'Oh, Guy — would you?' she implored. 'Redvers won't listen to a word I say and if things go on like this I think my heart will break. Can I stay here to-night? I can't stand the idea of going back to the cottage and finding Miranda there.'

'Yes, of course you can stay,' he said soothingly. 'Caroline will be home soon and between us we'll sort something out. Now, dry your tears and cheer up. I promise you everything's going to be all right.'

She gave a little sigh and, resting her head against his shoulder, she closed her eyes, nestling closer as he patted her cheek in a comfortably avuncular manner. Neither of them heard the car and the first thing they knew of Redvers's arrival was the flinging open of the door and the sound of his voice, taut with anger, ordering her to come home immediately.

It was Guy who stood up, the pressure of his hand on her shoulder urging her to stay where she was. 'She's not coming with you,' he said quietly. He was a short, stocky man, nowhere near Redvers's height, but, nonetheless, he succeeded in looking a very formidable adversary. 'Listen to reason,' he continued. 'You can't expect Sara to make your ex-fiancée welcome. If you

213

choose to bring Miranda to the cottage, that's your own affair, but you might bear in mind that the two of you spending the night alone together will give ample grounds for divorce.'

Sara caught her breath. Divorce had not entered her head and the idea of ending her marriage, almost as soon as it had begun, filled her with panic. Was this what Redvers wanted, she wondered. Could he have forgotten already those blissful nights when they slept in each other's arms? At her cry of protest his glance swept over her almost contemptuously.

'Divorce would hardly suit Sara's book,' he said in tones of ice. 'She's got a meal ticket out of me, which is what she wanted.'

'I told you, she's not coming with you,' Guy insisted, clenching his fists in a belligerent manner.

Both men were looking dangerous and, fearing a fight, Sara scrambled hastily to her feet. 'Leave it, Guy,' she said and, without waiting for further argument, she walked ahead of them to the car, waiting with set lips for Redvers to open the front passenger door for her. She had done with running away. Whatever challenge she had to meet she would face it with courage. And let Miranda beware! Redvers was her husband and she would fight tooth and claw to keep him, not because he was a meal ticket — she shuddered, remembering with what contempt he had said those words — no, not because he was a meal ticket but because he was the man she loved.

9

She waited until they were out of sight of the house and then put her hand on the steering-wheel. 'Please wait,' she said. 'I'm not going to the cottage with you until we get a few things straightened out.'

Unaccustomed to being spoken to in such an authoritative manner, he pulled the car into the side of the road and switched off the engine. 'Well?' he said unhelpfully. 'What is it you wish to discuss?'

'First of all, how long is Miranda staying?'

'I haven't the faintest idea,' he answered. His fingers were drumming a tattoo on the steering-wheel and his face was turned implacably away from her so that she could only see his stern profile.

'Redvers — why did you invite her?

Was it to punish me?'

'In point of fact I didn't invite her,' he replied. 'The first I heard of it was when she phoned from the airport.'

Sara digested this in silence, perceiving a ray of hope. The fact that he hadn't actually invited Miranda put a different complexion on the matter. 'Did she know we are married?' she asked.

'Apparently not. She seemed surprised when I told her.'

'But not upset enough — or tactful enough — to take the next plane home?'

Before he could reply a low-flying aircraft zoomed overhead, filling the air with an ear-splitting roar. Redvers went rigid and his hands gripped the steering-wheel so tightly that his knuckles showed white. Then, as the aircraft turned in a wide circle, preparatory to making a second sortie, he tore open the car door and stumbled into the roadway, his hands clamped to his ears and sweat pouring down his face. For a split second he stood rooted to the ground and then he started to run in a zigzag fashion before finally falling in a huddled heap into the ditch at the side of the road. Sara watched in horror, no other thought in her head but one of loving concern. Then she, too, stumbled out of the car and ran to kneel beside him, cradling him in her arms and murmuring words of comfort and endearment.

Not until the noise of the aircraft died away into the distance did he regain control of himself, and then he pushed her roughly aside, clearly ashamed of his weakness and angry that she should have been a witness to his humiliation.

'Redvers — are you all right?' she gasped.

'I'm perfectly all right,' he answered. 'Let's get on with the journey, shall we? Heaven knows we've had enough interruptions and Miranda will wonder what has become of us.'

Miranda, always Miranda. Even after

the soul-shattering experience he had just been through, the first word on his lips was Miranda. It brought home to Sara more forcibly than ever what she was up against. Clearly Redvers was still obsessed by the girl who had jilted him. He had tried in vain to put her out of his mind, had pretended to himself that he hated her for what she had done to him, and it now seemed likely he had only married Sara because he was afraid that, if he saw Miranda, he would fall in love with her all over again. Marrying Sara would prevent this from happening, or so he had thought, but Miranda had decided otherwise and she had forced the issue by coming to the island and making it impossible for him to avoid meeting her.

All too soon they arrived at the cottage and Sara had to steel herself to go inside and greet the unwelcome guest. Miranda, however, apparently didn't notice her chilly reception.

'How lovely to see you again,' she gushed. 'Where was it we last met?

Wasn't it at Isobel's dinner party? I little guessed you were the girl who was going to take my place in Redvers's life. Actually I thought you and Toby Gregson were going to pair up. I remember you were all over each other and I remarked to Claudia that it wouldn't be long before wedding bells were chiming. But you managed to do better for yourself, didn't you? I suppose congratulations are in order.'

Sara held on to her temper with the greatest difficulty. How dare Miranda insinuate she had ditched Toby in favour of a wealthier man. 'Thank you,' she said with cloying sweetness. 'You're too kind. Redvers, may I have a whisky?'

Sara never drank but he poured her a whisky without comment and then one for himself, which he downed in a single gulp. 'I thought we'd all go out for a meal,' he volunteered. 'We normally dine at midday and make do with a snack in the evening. Like Mother Hubbard, our cupboard is usually bare and Sara wasn't expecting another mouth to feed.'

'Oh, but a snack would suit me fine,' Miranda said. 'We had such a wonderful lunch — it was like old times, wasn't it, Redvers? Remember that darling little restaurant we used to go to in Hove? Their scampi was out of this world.' She rolled her eyes heavenwards. 'And there was that wonderful celebration lobster supper we had the day we got engaged.'

'I would prefer to eat out,' Sara interrupted. 'Actually I didn't have any lunch and I'm absolutely starving.'

Redvers shrugged. 'Fight it out between you,' he said, making no effort to hide his irritation, 'I've got some jobs to see to and I won't be back for a couple of hours.' He flung open the door and slammed it shut behind him, leaving the two girls bereft of speech. It was Miranda who recovered first.

'Redvers always had a temper,' she remarked, 'and, from what he told me, he has every right to be angry.'

'And what did he tell you?' Sara demanded, fighting for self-control. If Redvers had confided in Miranda about their quarrel she would find it hard to forgive.

'Oh — this and that.' Miranda's voice was elaborately casual. 'Chiefly about the unreliability of the post. I gather he didn't receive my first letter — I wonder why? I suppose you didn't have anything to do with it?' Sara winced and a satisfied expression crossed Miranda's face. 'Yes, I thought so. You're nothing but a nasty little cheat and I'm going to make you sorry you ever had the temerity to marry Redvers.'

A sudden chill struck Sara's heart. This was no empty threat — she was sure of that. Could it be that Miranda had a weapon she was going to use against her, a weapon which would widen even further the rift between herself and Redvers? 'I married Redvers because I love him,' she faltered.

'And why do you think he married

you?' came the instant retort.

'Because he loves me, of course.'

Miranda was quick to seize on the note of uncertainty in her voice. She gave a derisive laugh. '*When* did he ask you to marry him?' she demanded. 'Wasn't it *after* he received my second letter? Yes, I know it was, so don't bother to deny it — your face gives you away. When I wrote I told Redvers I was divorced and that I was still in love with him. I asked if we could arrange a meeting.'

'So — what?' Sara spoke in a husky whisper. 'The fact that he didn't reply to your letter and that he married *me*, shows what his feelings were.'

'Didn't it strike you he might be afraid of his feelings?' Miranda's voice was like silk. 'He still cares for me but he hasn't forgiven me for jilting him, so he used you as a shield. Don't you understand, you silly little fool? Redvers is a proud man and he's ashamed of his weakness in still loving me.'

A little moan escaped Sara's lips.

Miranda's version could well be true, because it was immediately after reading the second letter that Redvers had proposed marriage. 'Soon', he had said. 'It must be soon.' She had suspected at the time there was something behind his eagerness to clinch the matter, but she loved him so much she had put her fears behind her, and she was sure there had been nothing phoney about Redvers's behaviour on their honeymoon.

'I'm certain he isn't still in love with you,' she said, mustering her defences. 'And it wasn't *my* fault about the letter — it was Caroline's.'

Miranda raised an eyebrow. 'So Caroline was in it, too, was she? I'm not surprised. That woman always hated me. Well, I can't help feeling sorry for you, Sara. My advice to you is to get out as soon as possible. And let me warn you,' she added, with menace in her voice, 'if you don't go of your own free will I have the means to make you.'

Again that threat. A shiver of fear ran up and down Sara's spine and she put a hand to her head. 'I have a migraine,' she said with perfect truth, as zigzags of coloured lights began to dance in front of her eyes. 'I'll leave you and Redvers to entertain each other — in any case, I'm sure you'd rather have my room than my company.'

'I'm so sorry.' Miranda's mocking voice followed her as she tumbled upstairs. 'Can I bring you a hot drink or something?'

Sara paused with her hand on the banisters. 'No thank you,' she sobbed. 'Just stay away from me — both of you. That's all I ask.'

Reaching the top of the stairs she pushed open the bedroom door and closed it behind her, shutting her eyes against the evening sunlight which poured through the open window. Desperately she pulled the curtains across and, falling onto the bed, she buried her face in the pillow.

The next morning the tension had not lifted and, to add to the trauma, a dense fog had descended during the night, making it impossible for any of them to go outdoors. Redvers had lighted the fire because the cold seeped into every corner, and Miranda sat curled on the hearthrug, holding out her hands to the blaze. She had washed her hair and, as it dried, it formed a golden aura around her head, making her look like a sweetly innocent angel. Sara could not help wondering what Redvers was thinking as his gaze rested thoughtfully on the delectable figure of his ex-fiancée.

He was making a pretence of reading yesterday's newspaper but Sara was not deceived and she knew, by the drumming of his fingers on the arm of his chair, that his nerves were on edge. Presently he tossed the paper aside and, without a word of explanation, he went out into the kitchen.

'Perhaps he's gone to make some coffee,' Miranda remarked.

Sara shrugged. 'I doubt it,' she said. 'Not when he's got two women to fetch and carry for him.'

'Yes, he's bone lazy, isn't he?' Miranda yawned and stretched, revealing she had very little on beneath her bath robe. 'Caroline's fault, of course. She never allowed him to lift a finger.'

'*Allowed?*' There was hint of dryness in Sara's voice. 'I'd like to see anyone trying to stop Redvers doing what he wants to do.'

Miranda's eyes narrowed. 'For such a short acquaintance you seem to know him remarkably well,' she observed.

'I happen to be married to him,' Sara retorted.

'Only because you tricked him into it,' came the instant reply. 'It's perfectly obvious who Redvers prefers. He couldn't keep his eyes off me just now.'

'I daresay he was wondering exactly what you have on under that bath robe,' Sara remarked, 'though actually it doesn't leave much to the imagination.'

'All's fair in love and war,' Miranda reminded her, 'and that's what it is, isn't it, Sara? War to the knife.' She paused to give added weight to her words. 'When it comes to weapons, I rather fancy I have the edge on you.'

'Really?' Sara pretended to be disinterested but again she was conscious of a little prickle of fear. 'Redvers has been gone a long time. I'll go and see what's keeping him.'

'Sure you wouldn't like *me* to go?' The bath robe had slipped off Miranda's shoulders and she struck a provocative pose, her eyes full of spiteful mockery.

'I don't think so — you might catch cold.' The ice in Sara's voice showed her contempt and she was shaking with anger as she followed Redvers out to the kitchen.

He was standing by the window with his back towards her and she longed to go to him and put her arms round him but the thought of Miranda held her back.

'This damn fog,' he groaned. 'Even the helicopters will be grounded.'

Sara held her breath. Did this mean he was anxious to get rid of Miranda?

Tentatively she took a step forward but, before she could say anything, the door was flung open and Miranda flounced in.

'Do hurry up with that coffee,' she said.

Redvers made an angry gesture. 'See to it, will you, Sara?' he said. 'I'd better fetch some more wood for the fire.' He opened the back door, letting in a dense cloud of fog, and Miranda gave an exaggerated cough.

'I'll go upstairs and put on some more clothes,' she said. 'This cottage is like a morgue.'

Ten minutes later, when Sara carried the coffee tray into the living-room, Redvers was replenishing the fire and Miranda was sitting by the table, studying what appeared to be a scrapbook. Judging by the smirk on her face, the contents were giving her great pleasure and she flicked a malevolent glance in Sara's direction.

'What's that you've got there?' Redvers asked, more for something to say than because he was interested.

'A scrapbook of newspaper cuttings,' she answered. 'It's a hobby of mine and it makes fascinating reading on a foggy day. Listen to this. 'The engagement is announced between Redvers Armstrong of Abbotsfield Manor and Miranda Claire, daughter of . . . ' She broke off with a nostalgic sigh. 'What a wonderful time that was,' she continued reminiscently. 'Do you remember the parties we were asked to, the presents that were showered on us?'

'All of which had to be returned,' he pointed out with some asperity. 'I don't see any point in digging up the past.'

'Oh, but *I* do,' she said. 'My scrapbook's full of interesting snippets. How about this?' she continued, turning a page. 'Talented local actress stars in Coward play'. Weren't those amateur theatricals fun? I sometimes wish I'd gone on the stage professionally. I believe I'd have made a go of it.'

'I'm sure you would,' came the dry response. 'Play-acting is one of your many talents.'

The compliment was double-edged but she ignored the irony. 'Thank you, darling,' she purred. 'You were always my most appreciative audience. I remember you sat through every performance of 'Private Lives' and, on the last night, you sent me a bouquet that was out of this world.' She picked up a pressed flower and held it against her cheek. 'My most precious memento,' she murmured. 'This dead rose was one of the things that sparked off a major row between Ronnie and myself. He accused me of holding a torch for you, and of course he was right. I still do, and it burns as brightly as the Olympic flame.'

Redvers's face turned a dull red. 'Will you please stop it Miranda?' he said through set teeth. 'You might have some thought for Sara.'

'Heavens, yes! How very tactless of me.' Miranda gave a high-pitched giggle. 'To tell the truth I'd forgotten her existence.'

'That's a laugh!' Sara exclaimed. 'Isn't all this for my benefit?'

'Actually, there *is* something here that concerns you,' Miranda said. 'By a strange coincidence your name is mentioned, and your photograph printed, on the very same page as a photograph of myself. Quite a coincidence, don't you think? But then, life is full of coincidences — that's what makes it so interesting. I seem to remember I was opening a sale of work in aid of some charity, and it's a perfectly ghastly photo of me — don't you agree, Redvers?'

He took the scrapbook reluctantly, cursorily glancing at the relevant page before handing it back.

'Aren't you interested in what it says about Sara?' Miranda asked. 'When I was first introduced to her I thought her name rang a bell and I suppose I must have registered it in my sub-conscious. Sara Ravenscroft. Look,

Redvers — that's her, isn't it?' She stubbed her finger on the page and held it in front of him. ''Local hero comes home to heartbreak'. It doesn't make very nice reading, does it? Perhaps you'll be sorry now for what you said to me last night. Ramming it down my throat that I'd jilted you in your hour of need. Sara's every bit as bad as I am — worse in fact. Bernard's a paraplegic, so his need was greater than yours, yet she ran out on him without a qualm. So much for your precious little saint. The scandal drummed her out of town and she'd almost decided to change her name to Mrs Gregson when you and your nice fat bank account happened to come along. No wonder she sucked up to your mother. You've really been taken for a ride, haven't you, Redvers?'

The strident voice went on and on, assaulting Sara's ears like an electric drill and, all the while, Redvers stood as if transfixed, not uttering a single word. This was what Sara had dreaded would happen, that one day Redvers would discover what lay behind her flight from her home town and why she had invited no friends to their wedding. It would be useless to try to explain that the broken engagement hadn't been her fault — he hadn't listened to her when she told him she was not to blame for the missing letter, so why should he listen to her now?

With a cry of anguish she left the room and, wrenching open the front door, she stumbled out into the fog which closed behind her like a curtain. By the time Redvers realized she had left the house she had vanished completely and he had no idea in which direction she had gone. Visibility was almost nil and, if he hadn't known the way like the back of his hand, he would have become as disorientated as Sara, who struggled desperately on, conscious of nothing except a terrible chill in her heart which had nothing to do with the clammy dampness of the sea mist.

Hours later the feel of spongy turf

beneath her feet told her she had reached the Lower Moors and she knew the airport lay ahead of her, so she stumbled on in what she thought was the right direction, little realizing she was turning in a wide circle and coming perilously close to the rocks at Peninnis Head.

Presently she could hear the pounding of waves and feel the flung spray on her face and, what had once been one of her favourite walks, became a place of terror. She held out her arms in front of her, trying to push aside the wet curtain of fog that half blinded her and, foolishly blundering on, she felt her feet slip on the loose shale, causing her to lose her footing. She tried desperately to save herself and might have managed to claw her way to safety if a seagull hadn't flapped its wings in her face, tearing into shreds the last remnants of her sanity. She uttered a single shriek of terror before falling headlong onto a rocky shelf, where she lay, deeply unconscious, until she was found hours later by a search party which had been organized by a distraught Redvers, whose ravaged face showed Miranda more clearly than any words that her cunning schemes had come to nought.

One look at Sara, her ashen face, and her tumbled hair matted with blood, would have convinced the most casual observer that she needed skilled medical attention straightaway. The hospital was not geared to cope with serious head wounds and Guy offered to fly with her to the mainland, leaving Redvers to follow on a motor launch as quickly as possible.

'What do you take me for?' Redvers asked, brusquely brushing aside this suggestion. 'I'm going with her, of course.'

'But I thought ... ' Guy's voice trailed away as he saw the expression in Redvers's eyes. He doubted if his friend even remembered that the very sound of an aircraft nearly drove him insane, for he was too concerned with the welfare of the girl he loved to spare any thought for himself.

Mercifully the fog had cleared and the airport was working flat out to catch up with the backlog of flights which had been grounded for nearly twenty-four hours. The mercy flight took precedence over everything else and, as soon as the stretcher with its unconscious passenger had been loaded onto the helicopter, the gigantic rotor blades started whirring and, with a deafening roar of powerful engines, the aircraft lifted vertically and then zoomed off in the direction of the mainland.

In an incredibly short time the patient was transferred from Penzance to the neurosurgical unit at Frenchay Hospital where a successful emergency operation was performed and ten days later Redvers was overjoyed at the prospect of being able to take Sara home.

Relaxed and smiling he sat beside her in the specially chartered Sikorsky that was to carry them across Mount's Bay for the final leg of their journey. A word to the pilot was sufficient to make him change course and approach the airport from a northerly direction, flying low over St Mary's Roadstead, which was glittering in the evening sun. It was Gig Night and hundreds of sightseers were cramming boats or jostling for vantage points along the waterfront in order to watch the most exciting of all races. Csar, Golden Eagle, Bonnet, Shah and Silver Dolphin could easily be picked out and the pilot grinned and said he always put his money on Bonnet.

As they swung inland Sara turned to Redvers with shining eyes. 'Thank you,' she said. 'That was a wonderful homecoming.'

He pressed her hand. 'And later on this evening, if you're feeling up to it, we'll go for our favourite walk and watch the sun setting over the western rocks,' he promised.

Guy and Isobel were waiting for them at the airport but, much to Sara's relief, they declined Redvers's invitation to come into the cottage. All she wanted was to be alone with her husband so that she could discuss with him the events that had led to her precipitous flight which had so nearly ended in disaster.

'Are you tired after your journey?' he asked solicitously. 'Perhaps we'd better postpone our walk till another time.'

'I'm not tired,' she insisted.

'But you're looking pale and anxious.' With gentle fingers he smoothed out the frown that creased her brow. 'What's troubling you, Sara? It's not that ridiculous business with Miranda and her stupid scrapbook, is it? It's all over and done with and forgotten. When you were so ill I sent for your father and he told me the true version of what happened between you and Bernard. Not that I believed the cruel things that were said in the paper about you. It was wrong of you, Sara, not to confide in me. Surely it would have been more sensible to have told me the whole story instead of bottling it up inside you.'

'I was afraid you'd hate me,' she whispered. 'I knew you hadn't married me because you loved me and I thought Miranda's revelations would more than ever convince you I was the wicked, scheming creature you already believed me to be.'

'You knew *what*?' he barked. 'That I didn't marry you for love? You must be out of your mind. What other reason would I have for marrying you?'

'Desperation,' Sara whispered. 'You still loved Miranda but she had wounded your pride and you wanted to pay her out for the pain she had inflicted on you.' Her voice broke. 'You used me as a shield, Redvers, to protect yourself from your own weakness.'

He ran his hands through his hair in a distracted manner. 'I've never heard anything so ridiculous in all my life,' he exclaimed. 'Whatever put such a stupid idea into your head?'

'You proposed to me just after you received Miranda's second letter,' she replied. 'Don't you remember?'

'Miranda's letter had nothing to do with it,' he insisted. 'I believe I tore it up and threw it into the waste-paper basket, which was the best place for it. Reading her insincere phrases sickened me and made me realize how much I despised her.' Almost savagely he seized her by the shoulders and gazed deeply into her eyes. 'I love you, Sara,' he groaned. 'I love you. I love you. I love you. 'Till a' the seas gang dry, my dear, and rocks melt wi' the sun, I will love thee still, my dear, while the sands o' life shall run'.'

He kissed her lingeringly and with increasing passion until it felt as though her very soul was being drawn through her parted lips.

Controlling himself he let his mouth trail gently down the slender column of her neck till it came to rest in the small hollow at the base of her throat. 'Forgive me,' he murmured, putting her gently away from him. 'You're so precious to me — doubly precious since I nearly lost you. I suppose we had better go for that walk. It may help to cool me down a little.'

She smiled at him with infinite tenderness. 'No, Redvers,' she said in a gently teasing manner. 'I think we have better things to do than watch the sun go down.'

THE END